The Buckle

a novel by:
John W. Mangum

The Buckle

Copyright © 2011 by John W. Mangum

ISBN: 978-0-9840896-2-8

Edited by Harvey Stanbrough
Layout & design by Dan Grams

Running Iron Press

www.runningironpress.com

Dedicated to:
To the 2009 - 2010 sixth grade class at the
Colonel Smith Middle School,
Fort Huachuca, Arizona.

Chapter One
Dad

A dull thud resounded through the stall as the two-year old colt slammed me against the wall. He snorted then bolted to the corner of the stall, leaving me cursing the day of his birth as I struggled to my feet. A sharp pain shot through my rib cage with every breath. I was in agony trying to recall the events in my life that had brought me to this train wreck....

It was early morning 2002, Mom and I had just watched the crystal ball make it's annual decent in Time Square. The doorbell rang. Mom looked at me, startled. "Who could that be at this hour?" She walked toward the door and flipped on the porch light. She called out, "Who is it?"

"Chaplain Beeler and Colonel Cone. May we come in? It's extremely important that we speak with you." As they walked in Chaplain Beeler said, "Mrs. Roland, please sit down."

I remember Mom looking terrified. The chaplain said, "Mrs. Roland," "We learned late this evening that your husband was killed in action during a firefight in eastern Afghanistan. His team came under heavy hostile fire while on a reconnaissance patrol in an area controlled by enemy troops."

Mom's face turned pale. Her eyes began to fill with tears. She tried to speak, but there was only silence. Trying to comfort her I put my arm around her quaking shoulders and pulled her close. A low moan came from somewhere deep within her. The two officers tried to control their feelings.

Finally Colonel Cone said, "The reports we received stated that Master Sergeant Roland performed in a manner that prevented his entire team from being annihilated. A complete account of his actions is forthcoming. I want you to know this news has affected many of his fellow troopers, many of whom, including myself, served with him on previous operations. He was a dedicated soldier. We also want you to know we will be here to help you and your son during this difficult adjustment."

Mother could not respond. She looked up at Colonel Cone with a tearful but kind expression.

I responded to the colonel. "Thank you, Sir. We need to be alone now. We have a lot to discuss. This has been quite a shock for both of us."

"We understand," replied Chaplain Beeler. "I'll be in contact with you later today."

"Thank you both. Let me show you to the door."

"No, we can show ourselves out," Colonel

Cone said. "You stay here with your mother." With that the two officers left. We couldn't mutter a word. We just held each other and sobbed. Our Green Beret had met his fate.

Mom looked at me, tears running down her cheeks. "What are we going to do now?"

"I'm not sure. The only life I've known is Dad being in the army. Now he's gone and we're left to fend for ourselves. Maybe I should quit school and go to work."

"Son, I can't let you do something like that."

"Then how are we going to make it? The only people we know around here are military. All my friends at school have their own problems to deal with. Some have already gone through this."

"I need to call my folks and let them know about your father," Mom said. "Perhaps they'll have some suggestions for us. Even though we haven't been that close over the years, maybe they will understand our situation."

"That's a pretty good idea," I replied.

Muffled crying came from Mom's bedroom all through the night. Mercifully the sun finally began to filter through the pine-trees. I made my way to the kitchen and put on a pot of coffee. Mom walked in. "Good morning, Mom. Would you like a cup of coffee?"

"Yes, Tyler, I sure would. I'll need a lot of it

before this day is over I'm sure."

I took her favorite cup from the cabinet, then filled it with the hot steaming brew.

She slowly sipped from the cup. Her blue eyes were transfixed as she stared out the window above the kitchen sink. Finally she said, "What are we going to do now, Tyler? Your dad and I have been together eighteen years. He's always been there to take care of us. I don't know how I'll make it without him." She burst into tears. "What will we do now?"

"Mom, I've thought about it all night. I really think I should quit school and find a job."

She shook her head. "I'll not hear of that. You only have a year and a half left to finish high school. Don't even think about it. Your dad would haunt me the rest of my life if I let you pull a fool stunt like that." Mom continued to sip her coffee, then picked up her cell phone and called her folks in Douglas, Arizona. I left the kitchen, giving them time alone to work through an extremely difficult phone call.

Seeing how they hadn't spoken to each other in quite sometime, I was curious as to what was said when I walked back into the room. "How'd it go, Mom?"

As she looked at me her eyes again filled with tears. "They were exceptionally supportive. They asked me what arrangements had been made for his return. I told them I hadn't even thought about it. Dad said he and Mom would be catching a flight to see us in Fayetteville, North Carolina as soon as they could arrange everything. I was shocked at his response. In all my life I can't remember him ever being this concerned about me."

As we discussed our situation, the phone rang and I answered it. "Hello?" It was Chaplain Beeler. "Yes Sir, she's right here." I looked at Mom. "Mom, it's Chaplain Beeler. He wants to speak with you."

She took the phone. "Hello? Yes... we were just discussing that. Sure... we'll be there at three o'clock. Thank you, Sir. I appreciate that." Mom hung up and turned to me. "Chaplain Beeler wants us to come into his office at the chapel today at three. He has news about your 'dad's return to the United States. He wants to discuss the arrangements for his burial."

"Are you up to it, Mom?"

"Yes Tyler, I am. As much as it's tormenting me I know it's something that must be done. I appreciate your concern for me though. Just knowing I have your support will help me through all of this."

We were at the chapel by three o'clock. As we

walked in I looked up at the stained glass windows. I think for the first time I noticed the beautiful window with a Special Forces trooper inlay. I remember having tightness in my throat and barely being able to swallow, thinking about Dad and all of those who had given their lives in previous wars. It was an intensity I had never felt before. The emotional roller-coaster I was on only made me more determined to care for Mom and get us through this unbearable situation. I wouldn't quit school to flip burgers. I'd make something of myself and make her proud of me and honor the memory of my dad.

Chaplain Beeler walked into the chapel. "Welcome" he said. "Come into my office." When we were seated Chaplain Beeler told us that they expected Dad would be brought back to the United States within a week. He said the burial sight would be up to Mom to decide.

Mom asked, "Would it be possible to place him at Arlington?"

Chaplain Beeler nodded. "Under the circumstances I'm sure it would be possible."

Just like that, it was settled. Dad would be buried in Arlington National Cemetery with full military honors. I'll never forget leaving Chaplain Beeler's office. Dark clouds were forming and a cold misty breeze chilled us to the bone. Mom could barely hold back the tears as we walked to the car.

As we drove to the house she was extremely quiet, then she said, "It was strange trying to think of the best thing to do for your dad. I was wishing his folks could have been there to help me make decisions."

"What happened to them?" I asked.

She stared out the windshield for a long moment, then said. "Two years after your dad and I married they were driving to Phoenix. It was one of those windy, dusty days. Just out of Eloy blowing dust caused a multiple car accident. They were involved in the accident and killed."

"My gosh, Mom! I didn't realize that's what happened to them. I always wondered why Dad didn't speak of them much. I asked him about them once and he just said they were dead. He said he didn't want to talk about it, so I just dropped the subject."

"It was very hard on him," she said.

When we reached the house Mom went in and called her folks to let them know of the funeral arrangements.

Almost two weeks went by. Dad's body had been flown to Dover Military Mortuary, then to Andrews Air Force Base just outside of Washington D.C. He was then taken to Arlington

National Cemetery.

The day of the funeral we all met at the Custis Lee Mansion. My grandparents were extremely attentive of Mom that day as we were escorted to the gravesite. We were seated under an awning and a cold breeze wisped through the air. The deciduous trees had long since lost their leaves. Patches of snow covered the ground. Soon an honor guard arrived with a gray casket. An American Flag was draped over it, and the stark realization hit me: *My dad is in that coffin.*

As they placed the cold coffin on the stand over the grave I began to recall better times. Now all that remains are those precious memories. The chaplain said a final prayer and twenty-one precise rifle shots rang out. The haunting notes of a bugler sounding "Taps" compounded our every emotion. Someone presented Mom with the precisely folded American flag.

As we left Arlington I vowed I would return as often as possible to visit my dad, and others who had gone before and those who would surely follow.

On the trip back to Fayetteville, Granddad and Mom carried on a serious heart to heart conversation. By the time we reached the house it was decided that Mom and I would leave Fayetteville and our lives as military dependents and move to Douglas, Arizona. I thought, *What next?*

For the next two weeks my grandparents helped Mom get things in order at the bank and arrange for the move to Arizona. I helped pack our belongings and we rented a large U-Haul truck.

Chaplain Beeler had some soldiers come over to help load everything. He came by to see us the day we loaded the truck and told Mom he would stay in contact with her. He said that Dad had been recommended to receive a Silver Star and Purple Heart. I thought, *Dad already had a Bronze Star and a Purple Heart... what are we going to do with another one? I'd rather have my dad.*

The big day arrived and Granddad and I headed out in the truck and Mom and Grandmother followed in the car. I had no idea where I was going or what would be there when we arrived. I just knew my life would not be the same.

Chapter Two
Going West

In one of my U.S. History classes I had read a quote that Horace Greeley had made back around 1865: "Go West Young Man, and Grow Up With The Country." As my granddad and I drove toward the setting sun that first day I thought about that quote and wondered if it would be possible for me to grow with the West. For the first time in my life I was faced with the realization that I had to do something with my life that would benefit Mother and myself.

Neither of us were prepared for the fate that befell us. I really didn't know my grandparents all that well and I certainly new nothing about Douglas, Arizona. I decided the best way to get an understanding of everyone and everything was to start asking questions. After all it looked like we'd be on the road for at least four days.

Granddad seemed pretty easy to talk to so I started. I thought I'd first try to get an understanding of him and my grandmother. "Granddad, how long have you and Grandmother lived in Douglas?"

He looked over at me and smiled. "I wondered how long it would take for you to start asking questions. Your grandmother and I have lived there most of our lives. We went through all of our schooling in Douglas. When we graduated from high school she went off to Arizona State University. I decided I'd get a job at the smelter. I worked there a couple of years, then joined the service."

After awhile, I could tell by the look on his face and the tone in his voice my questions were starting to stir up some deep-seated memories. He would pause at times before answering, like he was unsure he really wanted to let that part of his life be known. He needed a break, so I stopped asking questions. He just sat there quietly, his jaws flexing as he clenched his teeth. It was like he was recalling things that were too painful to talk about.

About nine p.m. we pulled into Atlanta, Georgia. Granddad found a motel just off Interstate 20. "We'd better stop for the night and get something to eat. We have another long day ahead of us tomorrow. I'd like to make it to Shreveport or maybe even Ft. Worth tomorrow."

He was a person who planned everything down to the last pit stop. We had a nice supper and turned in. Lying there in the dark staring at the ceiling I recalled some of the things I'd learned that day. My Granddad must have lived a very interesting life. For a man in his sixties he was still pretty spry.

The next morning we had finished breakfast by 7:00 a.m. and were back on the road. I thought, *At this rate we just might make Ft. Worth today.* Granddad seemed preoccupied as we drove westward, so I started asking him questions again. "What sort of town is Douglas?"

He hesitated. "Well, it's not a bad little town. It used to have a lot more folks back in the '60s. Back then the largest employer in Douglas was the P.D. Smelter. There was a lot of farming just to the north in a little town called Elfrida. Ranching was a lot stronger back then also. However, the farming came on hard times and they closed the smelter. Things sort of went downhill after that. It's hard to say if Douglas will ever be the town it used to be."

As we drove along I began to wonder just what we were getting into. I was used to being around military towns like Fayetteville. Normally they were prosperous places to live. I wondered if Mom would be able to find a job in Douglas. The future seemed uncertain.

It had been a long day for sure. We did reach Ft. Worth and then drove to Weatherford, a town just west of Ft. Worth. Granddad said he wanted to get a fresh start in the morning away from the heavy traffic of Ft. Worth.

We headed west bright and early the next morning. I couldn't believe the horse ranches.

Some of them were just beautiful. Nice fences and the horses were grazing on green pastures. However, the farther west we went the more the terrain and vegetation changed. We went from grassy pastures to desert brush.

We finally stopped for the night in Midland, Texas. The next day we crossed into New Mexico, and then at Road Forks we left I-10 and headed to Douglas on Highway 80. When we turned onto Highway 80 I noticed a sign that said *Agua Prieta. What sort of name is that?* I wondered.

We made it into Douglas late that evening and went to my grandparents' house. We were all pretty tired. It had been a long trip. Getting through Texas seemed to take forever.

The next morning we were all sitting around the table having breakfast and discussing what to do next. Granddad said he wanted us to stay with them until we got adjusted to the area and found a house that suited us. He said we could store our belongings in their garage. Mom agreed and later that day we unloaded the U-Haul.

Monday arrived and Mom and I drove over to the high school. When we got there students were beginning to congregate in the halls and out on the front lawn. I could tell we were being watched as we walked up the sidewalk toward the offices. My insides felt like they were going to burst.

We finally made it to the office. A student

greeted us from behind the counter. "May I help you?"

"Yes," Mom replied. "Tyler would like to register for classes." Mom handed her the packet we had picked up at the high school in Fayetteville.

She took them from Mom. "Thank you. I'll get Mrs. Dunning." She turned and walked into an adjoining office.

A pleasant looking lady walked out with her. "Good morning. My name is Mrs. Dunning. I understand we have a new student to register."

I could tell by her smile and pleasant voice she was a kind person.

"Let's see here.... Fayetteville, North Carolina... my, you've come a long way! Looks like you have everything we need to get Tyler registered. I'll get one of the counselors to meet with you."

She walked down a short hallway and returned with a man in his late fifties. He walked up to us and shook our hands. "Good morning," he said. "I'm Mr. Hernandez. Please come into my office."

Mom and I followed him down the hallway to his office. It was a really cool office. He had loads of sports photographs on the walls and a beautiful saddle on a stand under photographs of what appeared to be young cowboys. Having never seen anything like that I stared at everything intently.

He must have seen I was curious about the saddle and photographs.

"Do you like rodeo?" he asked.

I hesitated, not knowing what to say. "Well, Sir, I never have been around rodeo before. I have ridden horses, but we rode English. Our saddles were much different."

He chuckled. "Yes, I guess they were. Well, our high school has a rodeo team. It's sponsored under the Agriculture and FFA program here at the school. In fact, the first Arizona High School State Championship Rodeo was sponsored by our Ag department back in 1962. For now, I guess we'd better get you registered." He looked over my transcripts. "Looks like you've already taken Algebra and Chemistry and done quite well in both. Actually, it looks like you've done well in all of your classes. Let me show you the classes you'll need to graduate here in Arizona." He began going over the required curriculum, then said, "We also have some great electives." He began naming the electives, including the agriculture classes and the FFA.

"Tell me about the agriculture classes," I said. "What exactly is the FFA?"

He laughed. "Well, it's actually called The National FFA Organization—Future Farmers of America—but it's about a lot more than farming. It's a co-educational organization for boys and girls interested in learning the many aspects of agri-business."

When all was said and done I ended up with four required classes and I had enrolled in the agriculture program with hopes of becoming a member of the FFA. I didn't know at the time how significant that would become in my life, but as fate would have it my life had been set on a new course.

We completed my enrollment and left Mr. Hernandez's office. I walked Mom out to her car, then returned to my first class. I can' t remember when I was so nervous. It wasn't like before when Dad was with us. I felt as though a big part of me was missing. Maybe it was the fact that I couldn't believe Dad wouldn't be with us anymore. Many mixed emotions raced through my mind as I walked into the classroom.

Mr. Jennings assigned me a desk, then said to the class, "We have a new student with us today." He looked over at me. "Tyler, why don't you come up and tell us where you're from and a little about yourself?" He chuckled. "I know the girls would really like this information."

Terrified is an understatement as to how I was feeling. I was about to burst, and now I had to get up in front of the class and tell them about myself. I slowly got up and walked to the front of the class. "My name is Tyler Roland. My mom and I just moved here from Fayetteville, North Carolina." I hesitated, then said, "My father—" The words stuck in my throat. Thoughts of what I had experienced over the past month raced through me. I tried to speak, but the words just weren't there. I hesitated and looked at Mr. Jennings. "Sir, would it be possible for me to do this some other time?"

"Perhaps another time would be better."

"Thank you, Sir." It seemed like a hundred eyes were staring at me as I walked back to my desk.

Classes seemed to drag by that morning. Thank God I wasn't asked by other teachers to tell about myself. Noon finally arrived and I made my way to the cafeteria. I went through the line, picked up my meal and found an empty table. I wasn't paying much attention to anyone.

Suddenly someone said, "Mind if I sit here with you?"

I looked up and saw a boy about my age. He had on what I called blue jeans. He was wearing a plaid shirt and for some strange reason he was wearing boots. I could tell he was in pretty good physical condition. He didn't have a speck of fat on him. *Must be an athlete*, I thought.

"Sure," I said. "Have a seat."

He held out is hand. "My name is Clay... Clay

Billings… What's yours?"

I shook his hand. "Tyler Roland."

He placed his tray on the table across from me and sat down. "Pleased to meet you. I was in your first period class this morning when Mr. Jennings asked you to speak to the class. I can't believe he did that to you on your first day. Seems to me just starting at a new school would be difficult, much less having to get up in front of a bunch of strangers and tell about yourself."

"Yeah," I said. "I felt pretty uneasy."

"What brought you to Douglas?" he asked.

"It's a long story," I said. "I lived in Fayetteville, North Carolina. My dad was in the service and stationed at Ft. Bragg. He was a career soldier. They're called lifers. He had been in for almost nineteen years."

"Where is he now?"

"Dead," I replied. "He was killed this past December 31st."

"My gosh, Tyler! How did that happen?"

"He had been deployed to Afghanistan with his team. They were on a patrol and he was killed during a firefight." Tears welled up and I paused, then looked over at Clay.

He was just staring at me, having a hard time believing what I had just told him. "I understand now why you couldn't do what Mister Jennings asked you to do this morning. You've been through a lot."

I wanted to change the subject. "What does your dad do?"

"He's a rancher. We have a ranch just northeast of town. We run black-baldies."

"What's that?"

"Well, we have Hereford and Angus cattle, and we cross breed them. About ninety percent of the time the calves are born with black bodies and white heads. That's why they're called black-baldies."

"Man, that's interesting!"

"Haven't you ever been around beef cattle?" he asked.

"No. All I've ever been around is the military. We were stationed at Ft. Bragg for quite awhile. Dad would have to leave from time to time, but Mom and I just stayed at our home in Fayetteville. I didn't do much except go to school and play sports."

We talked all through the lunch period. Clay was easy to talk to and I felt at ease getting to know him.

"What's your next class?" he asked.

"You're not going to believe this. I registered for the agriculture class. I was curious as to what it was all about."

"No joke? That's my next class too. Come on. I'll show how to get out to the Ag room."

We discarded our trays and walked toward the Ag building. As we walked I asked Clay to tell me what actually is involved in the FFA and the Vocational Agriculture program. After all I had never experienced anything like it before.

Clay was happy to explain. "The VoAg classes deal with various aspects of the agriculture business. Students developed projects related to agriculture. Some even work with chapter projects. In fact, our chapter has a Tilapia fish and hydroponic program right now."

Not knowing how I would fit in with all of that, I said, "Clay I'm sort of confused about projects. Do the students determine what they're going to do, or does the teacher assign them a project?"

"It's normally up to the student to determine what the project will be. Sometimes Miss. Griggs will help out."

"What do you do?"

"Well, since we have a cattle ranch, I have a few head of cows and a four Quarter Horses. I use one of the horses to rope on and the others are mares. I've sold some of their foals, but now and then we'll keep one. We break them and use them on the ranch."

I began to think that perhaps I was in over my head with this agriculture stuff. I'd never been around anything like this in my life. What would I do for a project? Would the other students accept me? Maybe the loss of my dad and having to relocate to a place whose culture was so different than what I was used to was overwhelming me. As we walked into the classroom, sweat was running down my back and it was probably only fifty degrees outside.

Clay seemed confused with my silence.

Chapter Three
Ag Class

As we walked into the building, Clay said, "Let me give you a quick tour of the classroom and the shop." The foyer walls were covered with photographs of former members from years past. He showed me the computer room where they worked on research and record keeping of their projects and activities. The shop was very well equipped with welding machines and tools they used for their shop classes. I knew right away that I was going to like this class.

Clay introduced me to some of his friends. It was a strange feeling, meeting these new people. It wasn't like other places 'I'd been. They made me feel welcome and I must have answered a dozen questions about myself before class started.

Soon Miss Griggs, the agriculture teacher and FFA advisor, came into the classroom. As she walked in she was reading a document. As she reached the podium at the front of the classroom, she looked up. "Looks like we have a new student." She looked at me smiled. "Tyler Roland, welcome to our class. I hope you will enjoy studying the many aspects of agribusiness that we explore. Would it be possible for you to stay a few minutes after class? I'd like to go over a few of things with you concerning what we do in our course of study and a little about The National FFA Organization."

"Yes Ma'am."

She began the day's lesson. I wondered whether I would really be able to understand everything she was explaining to us. I'd never had this sort of instruction before. I was used to the normal subjects like algebra, chemistry and other normal classroom work. I stayed after class and Miss Griggs gave me some study guides on the subjects we'd be covering. She also told me about the FFA and some of its' history.

I left the classroom with a lot on my mind. The biggest thing was trying to decide what I would do for a project. Clay had told me about his cattle and horses but that seemed out of reach. After all, I didn't have a ranch to raise cattle and horses on.

As I walked to the main campus, Clay approached me. "Well, what do you think?"

"It sure was different than anything I've ever done before. I just hope I can get something going on a project. I'm pretty concerned about that. I've never had anything to do with agribusiness before. It's totally new for me."

"Look, Tyler, I know you're really trying to fit in out here. Don't take it so seriously. There are a lot of guys and gals that will help you get the hang of things. We've all had to deal with getting started."

"Yeah," I said. "But it had to be a lot easier having been raised on a ranch that's been in your family for decades. I mean it was sort of a natural path for you. I was raised in a career military home."

He nodded. " I really respect you for all you've had to experience over the last little while. Man you've experienced something that none of us have even come close to. I don't know what I'd do if something happened to my dad."

"Thanks Clay. I appreciate your concern. Believe me, I plan to work this out. I want to learn something different. This might be what helps me overcome the lost feelings I've had since... well, since Dad was killed."

"Well, I'll do all I can to help you get a project started. I want to introduce you to my dad. We're planning on taking in a movie this weekend... would you like to go with us?"

"I'd have to clear it with Mom. Wouldn't you have to ask 'your dad if it would be all right with him if I came along?"

He laughed. "Yeah, but when I tell him I've got a new friend who just enrolled in school, it'll be all right with him. He knows I don't make friends with just anyone. He trusts my judgment."

"Well, okay then. I'll ask Mom about it. I'll let

you know tomorrow."

"Sounds good, amigo. I'll catch you tomorrow."

I watched Clay head for the bus stop. As he walked away he stopped and turned, then waved and yelled, "See'ya in the morning." I waved back and hollered back, "You bet."

I walked to the front of the school and there was Mom waiting to pick me up. When I got in the car she asked, "Well, how'd it go, Tyler?"

"It went well. I had some times, but all in all it went better than I thought it would. The agriculture class was really different. I truly enjoyed the kids in it and the teacher was very helpful. I met one fella that I really liked. His name is Clay Billings."

"Really?" Mom said. "Tell me about him."

"He lives on a cattle ranch. He has cattle of his own and horses. He showed me around and introduced me to others who were in the Ag class. He even asked me to go to the movies with him and his dad this weekend. Do you think that would be okay?"

"Are you sure about this boy? What are his folks like?"

"Well, if they're anything like Clay, they're fine people. Maybe I could introduce you when they pick me up."

"That's a good idea, Tyler. I look forward to

meeting them."

"Then it's okay to go with them?"

"Yes," she replied.

Mom wanted me to adjust to things, but I guess losing Dad made her more cautious than before.

That evening all of us were sitting at the table enjoying one of my favorites: fried chicken and mashed potatoes and gravy. Mom was not saying much, but suddenly broke her silence. "Dad?" she said. "Do you know the Billings family?"

Granddad looked up. "Sure do. They're one of the oldest families in Cochise County. In fact I think they settled here when Arizona was still a part of the New Mexico Territory. Why?"

"Well, Tyler met a young man at school today named Clay Billings."

"Oh." Granddad replied. "You must mean Pete Billing's son. Yeah, I know him... good kid." He then took another bite of mashed potatoes, hesitated, then asked, "What's up?"

Mom paused. "Well, he asked Tyler to go to the movies with him and his dad this Saturday evening. I just wanted to see what your opinion was of the family."

Granddad looked at her. "That's the kind of family you want Tyler to be around. They're hard working... good Americans. They mind their own business and help others when they can. You don't have to worry about Tyler being steered wrong by that family. No Ma'am, they're all right in my books."

"I'm relieved to hear that. I've already told Clay he could go with them. Thanks, Dad... you've set my mind at ease."

It was good to know that everyone was okay with the idea. Somehow I knew that meeting Clay was probably one of the best things that could have happened. I could hardly wait to see him the next day and let him know it was okay for me to go to the movies with him and his dad.

Trying to go to sleep that night, I thought about that first day at Douglas High School and the challenges I was facing. Not having Dad around would make it even more difficult. He was always there before to help me through things. Now I was on my own. I had my grandparents and Mom, but things seemed a lot different knowing Dad 'wouldn't to be there to talk things over with.

The alarm went off at 0600 and I hit the floor running. I couldn't wait to get to school and let Clay know I was given permission to go with him and his father to the movies. I also wanted to ask him more about his cattle and horses.

Mom dropped me off at school about the same time as Clay's bus arrived. I walked over and waited for him to get off the bus. "Morning Clay," I said. "How's it going?"

"Mornin' Tyler... things couldn't be better. What's new in your world today? Did you ask your mom about going to the movie this Saturday?"

"I sure did and she said it would be all right to go. Who all will be going?"

"Looks like just Dad, you and me. Mom has been under the weather lately so my sister Ginny is caring for her."

"I didn't know you had a sister."

"Yeah... she's a sophomore here. She stayed home with Mom today or I'd introduce her to you —another time I guess."

I grinned. "Man, you're full of surprises."

We walked over to Mr. Jennings classroom, just talking. ''When the bell sounded and we walked into the classroom, Mr. Jennings asked me to step out of the room with him for a minute. I couldn't figure out what I'd done, but I left the room with him. In the hallway he looked at me. "Tyler, I want to apologize for putting you on the spot yesterday in class. I had no idea at the time of your situation. I hope you will find it in your heart to forgive me."

I'll never forget the expression on his face. It took a big person, a person of good moral character, to do what he had just done. I accepted his apology and thanked him for his concern. Mr. Jennings became one of the best teachers I had while attending Douglas High School.

At the end of the day I walked over to the bus with Clay. Before he got on the bus, he said, "Tyler, I've got some ideas on your Ag project situation. Let me see what I can work out."

The rest of the week went by fairly well. I got to know a few more people and I definitely learned more about The National FFA Organization and all of the activities they participated in.

I began to really get excited about being in the FFA and I wanted to learn all I could about it. I also wanted to develop a good agriculture project. I didn't have the first clue as to what it would be, but it would be the best I could put together.

Chapter Four
Pete Billings

Saturday evening finally arrived. The movie seemed almost secondary at this point. I was really looking forward to meeting Clay's dad. From what Granddad told me he must be quite a cowboy. According to Granddad he rodeo'd and had a pretty nice ranching operation. I thought Clay was lucky to grow up in a situation like that.

A white pickup pulled into the driveway and Clay got out. A rather tall, medium built man wearing a nice hat came around from the driver's side. I was at the door as they walked up. "Hi there, Clay. Come on in."

Mom, Granddad and Grandmother walked into the living room. Clay looked at them. "Hello, my name is Clay Billings and this is my dad, Pete Billings."

" I've known Pete for a long time," Granddad said as he shook Mr. Billing's hand. "How y'doin', Pete?"

"Just fine, Mr. Sanders. How have you been?"

"Couldn't be better," Granddad replied. "You know my wife Martha and this is our daughter, Katherine Roland… she's Tyler's mom."

"Pleased to meet you, Mrs. Roland."

Clay spoke up. "Dad, this is my new friend

Tyler."

"I'm glad to finally meet you, Tyler," he said as he shook my hand. "Clay's told me a lot about you."

"I'm certainly pleased to meet you Sir." I replied. I couldn't believe I was finally meeting a real rancher. I wouldn't have been anymore star struck if I had just met Sam Elliott.

"Guess we better get to the theater," Mr. Billings said. "We don't want to be late."

"It was nice meeting you, Mr. Billings," Mom said.

"Just call me Pete," he said as we walked toward the front door.

"Thank you. You can call me Kay."

He turned and grinned at Mom. "I'll do that, Ma'am… I mean Kay."

As we walked toward the pickup Granddad called out, "It was good to see you two. Come back anytime."

It's been nine years since I met Mr. Billings that evening, but I'll never forget the conversation we had on the way to the theater.

"Clay tells me you've enrolled in the agriculture and FFA programs at school," Mr. Billings said.

"Yes Sir, I have."

"Clay told me you were troubled about putting together an Ag project."

"Well, yes Sir... I am pretty concerned about that part of it. You see, Sir, I've never been able to do something like this before. The classes I'm used to are just the normal ones like math and English... you know, stuff like that."

"Well, Clay and I have been discussing your situation this week. We've come up with a little plan that might help you. The plan really depends on whether or not you want to go along with it. Are you interested?"

"Sure."

"Well, you already know we're in the cattle business. Our family has been in these parts for a long time... since the late 1880s. We have a pretty sizable operation that requires a lot of work. We have a couple of full time hands, but when we brand calves in the spring and then ship them in October we need day hands. Also we ride and check the cattle a lot during the year and have to doctor some from time to time. We also do a lot of other things like putting out salt and supplemental feed. Then there are the water lines and tanks we have to check. So you see there's just a whole lot to ranching. It can be brutal at times. Anyway, we were just thinking that maybe you'd like to be one of our regular day hands. The pay isn't all that great. You'd probably make more bagging groceries at the Safeway, but you wouldn't have the experiences you'd get at the ranch."

"Mr. Billings, You don't know how much I'd like to work with you and Clay. This is like a dream come true."

Clay chimed in. "This is great! We'll even teach you to rope." He turned to his dad. "Won't we, Dad?"

"You bet... every cowboy needs to know how to use a rope. That's a given."

I thought I was having an out of body experience. How could I have been so lucky as to meet Clay and then have his dad accept me like that? I knew in my heart that I was about to embark on a unique experience. Little did I know at the time just how all of this would become a part of my life.

We caught the early evening show and then went to the Gadsden Hotel for some pie and coffee and to continue our conversation about me working at the ranch.

"When do you want to come out and check out our operation?" Mr. Billings asked.

"Well, Sir, I'll clear it with Mom tomorrow and let Clay know Monday at school. The sooner the better as far as I'm concerned."

"That sounds good to us," Mr. Billings said. "We look forward to you coming out."

We finished up our pie and coffee and they drove me back to Granddad's house. What an evening that had been! I couldn't wait to discuss everything that had gone on with Mom.

The next morning I walked into the kitchen. Mom and my grandparents were sitting at the table having their morning coffee. Mom looked up. "Well, how did it go last night? Did you enjoy the movie?"

"The movie was fine, but I have to tell you what Mr. Billings offered me. You probably know I've been very concerned about what to do for my agriculture class project."

"Yes, I know it's been worrisome for you."

"Well, Mr. Billings asked me if I'd be interested in doing part time work at their ranch. They call it being a day hand."

A concerned look flashed across Mom's face. She looked as though he had asked me to fly to the moon or something dangerous.

"He told me I'd be helping during the spring round-up and branding and then helping ship calves around October. I'd also be helping with the everyday sort of things like feeding livestock, checking water lines and helping with doctoring when needed. You know, ranch work."

"When is all this supposed to start?"

"They'd like me to come out and check things out as soon as I clear it with you."

Mom looked over at Granddad. "What do you think, Dad?"

Granddad paused for a minute. "I'll tell you one thing for sure, Kay. If Pete Billings offers a young green-horn a chance at a job like that, it's because he wants to help him out. This would be a good chance for Tyler to learn what it's like to earn a day's wages. That's something a lot of young people nowadays really don't understand. There's just not enough wood to chop. Kids get bored and that can lead to trouble. If it were me, I'd keep Tyler on that ranch every spare moment he has. It's for sure he couldn't be with better people."

"I guess that settles it," Mom said. "Looks like you're going to learn to be a cowboy." She chuckled. "Just remember when you come home, be sure to take your boots off at the door. From what I've heard they can get to smelling pretty rough working around cattle and horses."

Was I ever excited! I couldn't wait to get back to school on Monday and let Clay know Mom had agreed to me being a day hand.

When Clay got off the bus that Monday I was waiting.

"How'd it go?" he asked.

" After Granddad spoke up for me, Mom said it would be okay. I guess now we'd better figure out when I need to get started."

Clay smiled. "I think Dad had a gut feeling it would be a done deal. He told me to ask you if you'd like to come out to the ranch Friday after school. You could ride out with me on the bus."

"Man alive, Clay, it can't happen soon enough to suit me. Thanks, man… and please tell your dad thanks when you get home today."

After lunch Clay and I went to our vocational agriculture class. We spoke with Miss. Griggs and informed her of my plans to work for the Billings' Ranch. Clay told her his dad was making plans to teach me as much as he could about the cattle and horse business. She told us she thought that would be a great idea and that she thought it might help me determine what type of project I wanted to pursue.

The rest of that week seemed to drag by. The main thing I had on my mind was getting out to that ranch to start working and learning.

Granddad was getting into the idea too. One day after school he took me to a local saddle shop. That was a real treat. They had about everything a person would need to work on a ranch. Granddad bought me a good pair of work boots, a couple of pairs of Wranglers, work shirts and what he said might be the most important thing: some heavy leather gloves. The saddle maker showed me some tack and a saddle, but that was a little out of our price range that day.

Granddad seemed to be very knowledgeable

about what I would need to have for my new job. On the way back to the house after the shopping venture we had a very informative conversation. I asked him how it was that he knew so much about ranch work. To my surprise he told me he had worked on a ranch his grandfather had managed. He went on to tell me some of his adventures and how much he truly liked working there.

After I finished my homework that evening I relaxed in my bedroom and thought about some of the things Granddad had told me that day. I never would have expected that he had worked on a ranch. I'm sure that's why he spoke up for me. He knew working for Mr. Billings would test me. I guess he wanted to see if I had what it takes to stick with it.

The week seemed to drag by, and when Friday afternoon finally arrived it was all I could do to control my excitement. We were finally headed to the ranch.

Chapter Five
The Ranch

The ride to the bus stop seemed to take forever. We stopped at a wide spot in the road. There was an old pickup sitting off the road near what appeared to be a dirt road that headed north into some foothills. Behind them in the distance you could see that the foothills began to turn into full-fledged mountains. What we had called mountains back in North Carolina wouldn't begin to compare with these.

I was still transfixed looking at the mountains and the wide-open grassland leading into the foothills, when Clay said, "Well, here we are." I must have had a blank look on my face. He looked at me with a puzzled expression. "Are you okay Tyler?"

"Yes... Yes. I've just never seen country like this before."

Clay pointed. "That's my pickup over there. That's our ride to the house."

I thought, *This is really different. We ride a bus out here, get off in the middle of nowhere, then have to drive back into the hills to Clay's house in a thirty year old pickup.* I knew then and there that I needed a reality check. Two months ago I would have never dreamed this possible.

The pickup looked in pretty good condition for being as old as it was. We climbed in, and Clay put the key in the ignition and turned it. The old truck roared to life. It sounded like it should be in Daytona.

"What do you have in this thing?" I blurted out.

"Like that, do ya?" he replied. "It's a motor Dad and I put together in our spare time. It's an old 400 out of a GTO." Clay looked at me and chuckled. "Y'gotta watch her cause she'll fish tail out from under you if y'punch the gas pedal too hard."

Next thing I knew we were headed down that dirt road at a pretty good clip. Clay was cautious but he wasn't wasting any time. That little half-ton pickup had a lot of get up and go.

As we drove along I was looking at the country side. All of a sudden I saw some deer bounding away from the road. "Look! Those are the biggest deer I've ever seen."

"Yeah." Clay said. "Those are mule deer. There's a lot of 'em down here in the lower country. Back in those mountains the white tail are more numerous. We usually put in for this area every hunting season. We use venison to supplement the beef and pork we butcher every year."

I took it all in. I couldn't help thinking what a

different life style Clay lived. All I knew about the meat we ate was that we went to the super market once a week and bought it. Out here they raised their own and hunted deer. What a life!

We finally arrived at the ranch house. In the distance were barns and corrals. One of the barns was open on the sides and was full of hay. Some of the corrals had what appeared to be stalls next to them and there were two or three horses in them. I thought, *Man, this place is really well put together!*

"Well, we're here," Clay said as he opened the door to get out. I was almost speechless. I'd never seen anything like this before.

As we walked toward the house a dog ran up to Clay, glad to see him. As he knelt down the dog put his front paws on Clay's knee, and Clay began to pet him.

"This is Tobi," he said. "He's one of the best hands we have on the place. We never gather cattle without having him along to help."

"He sure likes you."

"We've been friends ever since he was born. His mom gave us a lot of good pups. About every neighbor within twenty miles has one or two of 'em. We have some friends over in Animas that even have some."

"You know, Clay, I've never had a friend like that. I've never even had a pet."

Clay looked up at me with a strange

expression on his face. "You mean you've never had a dog?"

"Nope." I said. "Not even a gold-fish."

He got up and slapped me on the shoulder. "Come on in, partner. I want to introduce you to my mom and sister Ginny."

I'll never forget the first time I walked into the ranch house. It was modest with western décor. Western prints depicting cowboys working cattle and riding broncs were neatly spaced on the walls. There were two cases of trophy buckles: one for Mr. Billings and one for Clay. I remember wondering how it would be to win something like that. There must have been a dozen in each case. I had never been in a home like this in my entire life.

Clay walked in with his mother and sister. "Tyler, this is my mother, Norma Billings."

She held out her hand. "Hello, Tyler. It's a pleasure to finally get to meet you. Pete and Clay have told me a lot about you. Welcome to our home."

I was tongue tied, I was so excited. "Th-thank you, Ma'am," I stuttered. It truly is a pleasure to be here."

"And this is the sister I told you I had," Clay said.

She spoke up. "I'm Ginny." She turned and looked at Clay. "Thanks Clay... You could have at least told him my name."

"Where's Dad?" Clay asked.

His mom said, "He's out checking the waterline in the horse pasture. He should be in pretty soon. He asked me to have you check those calves at the barn. They'll need feeding."

"Sure, Mom." Clay replied. "I'll change clothes and get down there. Come on, Tyler. You'll need to change out of those school clothes too. It can get pretty dusty down there."

We changed out of our good clothes and headed down to the barn. I had no idea what all had to be done.

My first time down at the barn area was memorable. The barn was well kept. There were four horses, some chickens running around and those two calves we were supposed to check on.

Clay went right to work preparing some sort of milky substances and putting it into a couple of large plastic bottles that had huge nipples on them, sort of like baby bottles on steroids.

"What the heck are you gonna do, Clay?"

"These are doggie calves. Their mothers were killed somehow. We found them and brought them in so we could try to save 'em… they're doin' pretty good."

"Yeah, but what are those?" I pointed to the large plastic bottles.

"Oh, we use these to feed 'em. This is a milk

replacer I put in them. We have to give them this until their digestive system can handle grass or hay."

He went over to a couple of racks that were secured to the fence and placed the plastic bottles in them with the large nipples pointed downward. "There he said. That should do it."

The two black calves with white heads walked over to the bottles and began nursing from them. "I've never seen anything like that before in my entire life," I said.

"That's why Dad and I wanted you out here. We want to teach you all we possibly can about living and working on a cattle ranch. This is just one of those things you have to deal with from time to time, especially this time of year when we're calving."

I listened to Clay talk, watching him go about his work so effortlessly. Would I ever be able to learn all of this? He pitched some hay to the horses and then checked all of the water troughs.

"Come on." He motioned to the corner of the barn. When we got there the wall of the barn had what appeared to be nests. He picked up an empty coffee can and began taking eggs out of the nests. "This is how we get our eggs, Tyler. There are a lot of kids at school who don't know those eggs in a store carton actually come from chickens.

"Out here we either grow what we eat in a

garden every spring and summer or raise it. We do buy some things at a grocery store in town, but not a lot. Dad usually milks our Holstein cow in the morning and it's my job to milk her in the evening."

"You folks sure know how to take care of yourselves," I said.

"It's been that way long before I was born," Clay replied. "My granddad taught Dad how things were done this way and I guess I'll do the same for my kids. It's not always glamorous living on a ranch—it's tough sometimes—but I wouldn't trade the lifestyle for anything. I love this land and I'll do all I can to preserve it for others to enjoy in the future."

I thought about what Clay was saying and began to really appreciate his philosophy. I remember thinking that more people should understand this. Maybe there would be less dependence on government. This made me realize that Mr. Billings and Clay were giving me the opportunity to learn self-reliance as well as helping me with my agriculture program for school.

The trip out here to the ranch also made me realize that I had a lot to learn. This wasn't going to be an overnight learning experience.

We heard what sounded like a Jeep coming toward the barn. "What's that?" I asked.

"Sounds like Dad coming back from the horse

pasture."

We walked out of the barn as Mr. Billings drove up in an old C J-7 Jeep.

"Howdy, boys." He called out. "What's goin' on with you two?"

"We've taken care of those doggie calves and done a few other chores," Clay answered.

Mr. Billings looked at me and grinned. "Glad you could make it out. I was wondering if you'd make it."

"Yes, Sir. I've really been looking forward to this."

"I'm glad."

"Clay, did you milk old Sarah-Bell yet?" He asked.

"Not yet, Dad. I was just about to get started on that when we heard you driving up. I'll get to it. Come on, Tyler. I'll show you how to milk a cow."

When Clay had finished milking the Holstein, we headed up to the house. It was getting dusk and the sun was disappearing over the hills to the west of the ranch house. A dim glow appeared through trees along the crest of the hills. It was a peacefulness I had never experienced.

When we entered the house Clay took the bucket of fresh milk that Sarah-Bell had rendered into the kitchen. I was in the living room when

Clay yelled, "Come on in here, Tyler."

As I walked into the kitchen, the aroma of freshly baked bread filled my nostrils. Mrs. Billings and Ginny were busy setting the table with a feast of pork chops, mashed potatoes and gravy, corn and that freshly baked bread. Glasses of sweet iced tea were at each place setting.

"Come on, Tyler. Let's get washed up," Clay said.

"You boys hurry up now," Mrs. Billings said.

I tried minding my manners by not eating too much, but Mrs. Billings kept insisting that I have more. She really didn't have to twist my arm. When I finally got up from the table after having some freshly baked apple pie with ice cream, I was stuffed.

"Thank you, Mrs. Billings," I said. That was truly a fine meal and that pie was some of the best I've ever eaten."

"You'll have to give Ginny credit for the pie," she said. "She's working hard to improve her baking skills for the FFA/4-H bake sale coming up at the Fairgrounds."

"Ginny, you should do real well selling pie like that," I said.

Ginny looked at me smiled. "Why, thank you, Tyler. I appreciate that."

Clay and I walked into the living room where Mr. Billings was sitting. He was reading what appeared to be an agricultural bulletin. "Have a seat, boys," he said. "I was just reading where the cattle futures are looking up. Maybe this year we'll be able to contract our calves at a pretty good price."

"That sounds good for a change," Clay replied. "What do you have in mind for us to do this weekend, Dad?"

Mr. Billings looked at me. "Tyler, you've ridden before haven't you?"

"Yes Sir." I replied. "But it was English style of riding. At one of the bases where Dad was stationed they were trying to teach us how to play polo. I enjoyed riding, but I really didn't like polo."

"That's not an easy sport to master, that's for sure," Mr. Billings replied. "But you at least learned how to handle a horse pretty well, didn't you?"

"Yes Sir, pretty well I guess. I rode at least three times a week for about four months. By the time we transferred to Ft. Bragg, I could do a lot on one. It came sort'a natural to me."

"How long ago was that?" he asked.

"Well, we left Fort Carson about three years ago. That was the last time I rode"

"Good. You should do all right. It's sort'a like riding a bike; once you learn, it don't take long to get back at it. Tell y'what, boys. I was thinking tomorrow we'd ride back into horseshoe and check the cattle up there. I'd like to look the calves over. Whaddya think, Clay?"

"Sounds good to me, Dad." Clay replied. "Tyler can start learning the country. He'll need to get to know it well if he's gonna work out here, that's for sure. What do you say, Tyler?"

I looked over at both of them. "Sounds like a winner to me."

We turned in early that night. The next day would be another new experience for me for sure. As we walked into Clay's room I was taken aback by the way he had it set up.

There were two twin beds with headboards that looked like they were made out of tree limbs. The chest of drawers was made of oak, and the closet was cedar lined. There was a five-point buck mounted on one wall. Photographs of Clay roping and riding bucking horses and bulls were on another wall. Some were of him receiving buckles and in one he was getting a saddle and a buckle. I wondered how it would be to win a buckle, or better yet a saddle and a buckle. It was beyond my wildest dreams.

Right then and there I set my goal to win a buckle. I didn't know how I was going to do it, but I was going to. My mind was made up.

We were up before dawn the next morning. Mrs. Billings and Ginny had prepared a fine breakfast of fresh baked biscuits, eggs, and bacon. We washed it all down with fresh brewed coffee. Was it ever a tasty breakfast! I knew if I kept eating like that I'd weigh a hundred ninety pounds real fast, but I learned later that you work it off pretty fast on a ranch.

We rode through the cows and calves that day. Mr. Billings kept taking a small spiral note pad out of his vest pocket and writing down things about the cattle as we rode along. I was curious as to what he was writing down. I asked him about it and he told me he was keeping track of the number of heifers and bull calves there were.

That piqued my curiosity. "Mr. Billings, why is that important?"

"Well, the price on heifers and steers is different. I also want to have an idea of how many calves we'll have to cut when we brand."

Clay spoke up. "We have to castrate the bull calves. If we don't the buyers will dock us on the price."

"Why do they do that?" I asked.

"Well, the buyers ship the calves to pasture somewhere and then to a feed yard where they're fattened up for beef. Steers gain weight and have better marbling in the meat, so it's tender."

Will I ever learn all of this? I wondered.

The next day we saddled up again and rode to another pasture checking calves. Mr. Billings continued to write information in his little spiral notebook. He and clay told me more and more about the operation. We must have ridden over at least two square miles.

By the time Monday morning rolled around I was tired but ready to come back for more. We were up early because we had to be at the bus stop by 5:30 a.m. Mrs. Billings had again prepared a nice breakfast for us.

However, there was a slight change when we walked out to Clay's pickup. Ginny was with us.

Chapter Six
Granddad

The ride back to school that Monday morning seemed to take less time than the ride out to the bus stop the previous Friday. To say I was disappointed having to leave the ranch would have been an understatement.

That week Clay and I spent a lot of time talking about the ranch and the work that they did out there. It was like he was schooling me away from the actual work. I must say I took it all in and tried hard to remember everything he told me.

I was able to talk with Miss Griggs more that week. She talked to me about what FFA activities I should be looking forward to for the rest of the semester. I told her that Mr. Billings and Clay had offered to give me work at their ranch. She told me that Mr. Billings had called her and gone over some ideas he had for me as far as my VoAg project. She didn't say much about their conversation, only that she looked forward to seeing me progress in the Vocational Agriculture and FFA programs.

After that first weekend out at the Billings ranch my Granddad had a lot he wanted to talk to me about. When I got home from school that Monday afternoon he had an old photo album he wanted to show me.

"Come in here at sit a spell, Tyler," Granddad said. "Remember I was telling you about my grandfather managing a ranch when I was about your age?"

"Yes Sir."

"This old album has a lot of photographs that were taken back then. Would you like to see 'em?"

"Sure, Granddad... I'd love to."

We sat next to the fireplace. There was a warm glow coming through the glass doors shielding the room from the fire. Granddad turned on a lamp and opened the photo album.

He pointed to a photo on the first page. "This was my Granddad when he first started to cowboy on the CO Ranch just east of Rodeo, New Mexico."

"He looks pretty young."

"He was about the same age as you," Granddad said. "He had to leave school to help support his mom and two sisters."

"Where was his dad?"

"His father had been working on the CO for about twelve years. He had gone over to El Paso to buy bulls. They say he was having terrible heart burn one evening after eating some red chili con carne. They tried to get him to get it checked, but being the hard head he was, he didn't. Later that night he fell over dead with a heart attack. Guess he'd had a bad heart ever since he got back from the Spanish-American War in 1900. He just never said anything about it.

"Anyhow, my Granddad Booker quit school and went to work for the outfit his dad worked for. He was fifteen. They lived there on the ranch. It wasn't much of a transition for him. He just didn't go to school any more."

"He eventually became the manager of the ranch and worked there until he died in 1965."

"How old were you when you worked there?" I asked.

"I started when I was about thirteen, working weekends, holidays and summers, right up to when I graduated from high school in 1962. I learned a lot working out there. It was a great life at times and at other times it was pure misery."

As he went through that old photo album I could tell by the way he talked that he had led quite a life. He would pause at times and seemed to drift, as though he was recalling images of days long since gone. Listening to him and looking at the photographs I learned a great deal about my family. Things I never would have imagined. It was clear to me that Granddad knew what he was talking about when it came to working on a ranch.

The following Sunday morning we were having breakfast when Granddad looked over at me. "How about just you and me going for a little ride today?"

"Sure," I replied. "Where are we going?"

"I'd just like to show you some of the country around here. You haven't had much time to really see much of it. It's just good to know the lay of the land."

We piled into his pickup with plenty of water and some sandwiches and headed east. I noticed Granddad brought along a rifle and what appeared to be a cowboy gun. When I asked him about them he just told me that things along the border were sometimes dangerous, that there was a lot of illegal activity. Being from Fayetteville, North Carolina, I couldn't imagine what could be so dangerous out here.

As we drove along we passed a small airport and I asked him about it. He said it was the oldest international airport in Arizona and maybe the oldest in the United States.

We continued east and eventually hit a dirt road. After some miles and time had passed he said, "That ranch over there is the old John Slaughter Ranch. It's a historical site now."

He said it like I should know who John Slaughter was, which I didn't. "Who was John Slaughter Granddad?"

He looked over at me. "You've never heard of John Slaughter?"

"No."

"My gosh, Tyler. What did they teach you about history back there?"

"Well, they never told us who John Slaughter was."

"John Slaughter was one of the toughest sheriffs in Cochise County. Some say he was even tougher than Wyatt Earp." Granddad said with a high pitch tone. "You do know who Wyatt Earp was… don't you?"

"I saw a film about him a couple of years ago," I said. "He was some lawman in the West who killed a bunch of cowboys… wasn't he?"

"Well, they need to make a movie about John Slaughter. Then you'd see what kind a man he was. He served in the Confederate Army during the Civil War, then moved out here and became a cattleman and sheriff. Even old Geronimo gave him plenty of room when he traveled through this country on his raids in Mexico and the United States."

"Sounds like a pretty tough man," I said.

As we drove along Granddad told me stories about the area and how Apaches and bandits would cross into Mexico. Then I found out why he'd brought his rifle and pistol along. He got a serious look on his face. "This part of Arizona and New Mexico is getting pretty dangerous again. Instead of Apaches and bandits, there are drug and human smugglers coming through here. Ranchers on both sides of the line are having problems with them."

We drove into New Mexico, and Granddad showed me a beautiful area he called Cloverdale. Then we drove into the little town of Animas. We drove out to what he said was left of the CO ranch where he had worked for his granddad.

I was beginning to get an idea of how the photographs he'd shown me the day before tied into what I saw that day. That was quite an experience. Not only had I learned a great deal about the country, I had also learned a lot of the history in that area and about how my family came to be a part of it. I had never thought about the importance of my ancestors until that day. It made me realize there was more to life than just what we were faced with now.

Granddad had his way of getting things across. As I look back on that day and others we had together, I'm thankful I was able to spend time with him.

For the next three weeks, we were trying to locate a house that Mom and I could move into. She felt that Granddad and Grandmother needed their privacy back. Looking back I guess it was quite a shock after all those years to have their daughter and grandson living with them.

During that time in agriculture class we studied various diseases that were common to livestock in Arizona. Miss Griggs really knew the subject well. She presented things in such a way that we were able to understand the symptoms and treatments for various diseases in cattle, horses, sheep and swine. Also, a guest speaker from a livestock pharmaceutical company gave us information on various vaccines used to prevent some of the diseases we learned about. The course ended with a veterinarian speaking to us on treating diseases. For some reason, I began to develop a strong interest in these subjects.

Our text books gave good information on them, but hearing the veterinarian explain the various aspects of treating diseases set a course that I wanted to follow, perhaps for the rest of my life. I began to study other aspects of veterinary medicine on my computer in the evenings.

Chapter Seven
My First Branding

Clay asked me if I'd like to get back out to the ranch. He told me they were going to start branding calves and I could start earning some day wages. I thought that would be great. I could also apply what we had learned in class. I was ready for that. I hadn't been out to the ranch for about three weeks. It would be good to get back.

Off and on that week, Clay talked to me about what we'd be doing. He wanted me to be aware of some of the jobs involved in branding. I was trying to remember all of it but must have seemed confused. He told me not to worry about it, and that I'd catch on in time.

Friday after school Mom was there at the bus stop with my duffle bag. Clay and I walked over to the car to get it.

"Hello, Mrs. Roland," Clay said. "How are you doing today?"

"Fine, Clay," she said.

About that time Ginny walked up. Clay said, "Mrs. Roland, this is my sister Ginny."

"I'm pleased to meet you, Ginny." Mom shook Ginny's hand.

"Likewise, I'm sure," Ginny replied.

"Sounds like you all have a big weekend ahead

of you," Mom said.

"Yes, Ma'am," Clay replied. "We're starting the spring branding. It will be two to three weeks of steady work. This weekend we'll gather and brand a few, but next week Dad and our hired hands will gather about three hundred head. We'll start on them next Saturday."

"That sounds like a lot of work," Mom replied.

"Yes, Ma'am, it will be for sure. Dad wanted me to ask you if Tyler could come out next weekend and give us a hand too, seeing as how we'll be out of school the following week for spring break. We could sure use the help and Tyler could pick up some good wages."

Mom looked at me. "What do you think, Tyler?"

"You know what I think, Mom. I'm ready."

"Well, then it's settled. I'll make sure you have plenty of work clothes ready. Clay, let your dad know he has another worker." Mom looked at me. "Just be careful and do as you're told."

"Yes, Ma'am. I will."

About that time the bus drove up and Mr. Frisky opened the doors. "All aboard!" he called out.

"Well, you better get going or you'll miss your ride," Mom said.

I gave her a hug and a kiss on the cheek. "Thanks, Mom. This means a great deal to me."

"You just mind your manners, Tyler."

As Clay, Ginny and I boarded the bus, I thought, *This couldn't get any better*.

That weekend I was introduced to real ranch work. Not only was it continuous, but it was physically demanding.

Saturday morning started at four a.m. We were up and having a nice country breakfast two hours before the sun came up. Our horses were saddled and we were heading for the home pasture just as a glimmer of light was glowing over the hills to the east.

When we reached the pasture Clay rode up and opened the barbed-wire gate. As I rode by him he looked up at me with a grin. "You're gonna start learning how to be a cowboy today, Tyler."

"Sounds like a winner to me," I replied.

Clay closed the gate and Mr. Billings asked us to gather round. He looked at me. "Tyler, this is your first time to gather cattle, so here's what we're gonna do. We'll split up and head to the backside of the pasture looking for cattle as we go. Once we hit the fence line we'll start back to this gate with all of them we can gather. This isn't a very big pasture so we should be able to gather about everything we have in here. I want you to ride along with me so I can explain what needs to be done as we drive the cattle this way."

"Where do you want us to go, Dad?" Clay

asked.

"Clay, you go on over to the north corner. Tyler and I will go to the south corner. Ernesto, you and Diego spread out between us. Let's push everything to the center of the pasture and head 'em this way."

Mr. Billings was very direct when giving us our orders. He'd done this many times over the years. During that ride to the backside of the pasture Mr. Billings explained how things were to be done. "Don't separate the cows from their calves. Keep them bunched and moving at a nice, steady walk, and for sure don't let them turn back on us."

It was like being in a classroom in a big open pasture on horseback. However, I knew that Mr. Billings was really trying to help me learn the ropes.

By midmorning we had begun to pull all of the cattle we'd gathered together into a large herd. Mr. Billings led the way toward the barbed-wire gate while the rest of us drove the cattle. Ernesto and Diego seemed to know automatically to stay on each side of the herd and prevented any of them from turning back. Clay and I stayed back and kept them moving.

I was very observant as to how they all seemed to know exactly what to do. I was getting a first-hand education. Dad used to tell me about On The Job Training. This was cowboy OJT for sure, and I loved every moment of it.

It was a little after ten a.m. by the time we pushed the cattle into the big railroad-tie-and-board-fence corral. As we drove them in Mr. Billings and Ernesto counted them. As the last pairs went through the gate, Clay yelled out. "How many are there, Dad?"

"I counted a hundred and eight head of cows." He looked over at Ernesto. "What did you get?"

"I got the same, Mr. Billings," Ernesto replied.

"That should be all we had in that pasture," Dad said. "Let's let 'em settle out a little before we cut the calves off."

We all rode over and tied up our horses in a small corral next to the working pens. Mr. Billings took his canteen off his saddle and walked back to look at the cattle. "Hey Clay, Tyler, come over here with me."

Clay and I walked over to the fence where Mr. Billings was standing looking through an opening between two of the two-by-twelve boards that were nailed to the railroad ties.

As we looked into the large pen of cattle, Mr. Billings said, "Tyler, I know Clay told you a little about the type of cattle we run out here. I'd just like to ad a little bit more to what he's told you. We breed these Black Baldies for a number of reasons. The cows are great mothers and they produce good milk for their calves. Cows like these usually take on the Hereford's foraging traits and do well on our type of country. Black Baldy calves sell well due to their ability to gain on grass as well as in a feed yard. When we buy replacement heifers we buy Angus, then breed them to our Hereford bulls. Then the calves are smaller, which cuts down on calving problems." He paused for a minute, then said, "There's a lot you're going to need to learn if you're gonna be part of this outfit."

I couldn't believe what he had just said. *Me? Part of their ranch?* I'd never been a part of anything before, much less something of this magnitude. I couldn't believe my ears.

Mr. Billings continued. "Clay and I have been discussing your situation with your VoAg project. We wanted to discuss it with you this weekend. Would you like to hear what we've come up with?"

Again I was taken aback. "Sure!" I was eager to hear what they were going to say.

"First off, before you can accept any of this, you're going to have to okay it with your Mother."

"Yes Sir, I understand. Mom and I have talked over about everything we've done lately. I mean, after Dad was killed, we've had to rely on each other for about everything."

"That's good. Well, with that out of the way let's get down to business. Clay you jump in with anything I forget that we've talked about."

"Okay, Dad. Go ahead. I'll just listen."

"Tyler, after Clay came home and told me about what happened to your family, I felt we should do something to help you get on the right track. It seems to us that you're interested in this sort of thing."

"Yes Sir, I really am!" I blurted out.

"Well...." "What Dad's trying to say, Tyler, is that we want to help you get started with your agriculture project."

"Yeah," Mr. Billings said. "We have some ideas you might like. We're gonna give you six of these cows and their calves. You'll get the proceeds from the sale of the calves. However, we'd like half of what they bring as payment. The other half is yours. The cows are already bred back so next year you'll get the proceeds from all of them you sell."

"You mean this?" I said.

"Hold on. There's a kicker in this deal," Mr. Billings said. "The money you get this year and next year for the calves has to go into an account for college. You can't just blow it on frivolous things."

Clay said, "Remember, Dad, he has to pay you a grazing fee."

"Oh yeah," Mr. Billings said. "We want you to pay four dollars a month per cow-calf unit. That'll be about twenty-four dollars a month, payable upon the sale of each calf crop. Also, starting today we'll pay you $50.00 a day wages when you're out here working. There's no strings attached to your wages. Whaddya say?"

I remember standing by that fence trying to put it all into perspective. I couldn't believe what I had heard. It seemed like it took me forever to reply. "Mr. Billings... I... I don't know exactly what to say. You hardly know me, and you're willing to do something like this?"

"Yeah, well... we figure you to be an all right sort. We just want to help y'out a little. It's not going to be all fun and games out here. You're about to get an idea of how hard some of this work is. Today's branding will be your first real day at cowboy tech."

Mr. Billings was right about that. We started cutting the calves off their mothers about 11:30, and Mrs. Billings and Ginny brought out a nice lunch about the time we had all the calves separated. I don't remember ever having a lunch that tasted better.

The working pens were set up well. They had a calf table they used to work the calves on. I'd never seen one of them before, but I learned the mechanics of it pretty fast. Our job was to keep the calves moving up the chute leading to the calf table. Mr. Billings, Ernesto and Diego worked on the calves. I saw them using their syringes for the vaccines we had learned about in Ag class. It made me realize how important it was to learn all I could in class so I could apply it out here on the ranch.

There were a dozen or so larger calves they had to drag to the fire. Ernesto would heel them and drag them to us. That's when I really learned how tough some of this work could be. Diego and Clay showed me how to flank the calves and hold them down to be branded. Most were bulls so they had to castrate them. I'll never forget that day. The smell of the smoke from the burnt hair was hard to get used to, and trying to hold the calves down was back breaking.

We finished branding just as it was getting dusk and turned the calves in with the cows. Diego and Ernesto put out hay for them in the large corral. Mr. Billings wanted to keep them there until the next day to make sure none of the calves continued to bleed.

We rode back to the barn and unsaddled. It was getting dark and the air was a bit chilly. We put the horses up and walked to the house. I remember walking in and smelling freshly baked bread. Mrs. Billings and Ginny had prepared a great meal. Ginny had baked another great apple pie for desert.

Ernesto and Diego came up to the house and

we all sat down at the big table for a grand feast of pot roast, mashed potatoes and gravy, green beans, fresh rolls, iced tea and apple pie. There wasn't a lot of conversation around the table. Most of the sound was five hungry cowboys chewing.

The next morning we rode out to the working pens and walked our horses through the herd. After Mr. Billings inspected the calves we drove them back to the pasture we had gathered them from. It was a slow trip. The calves were tired and sore. Reaching the dirt tank, we began scattering the cows and calves close to the water.

We moved away from the cattle, then just sat on our horses and watched. Some of the cattle drank profusely. A few of the calves found tuffs of dry grass to lay in.

I watched Mr. Billings closely. He seemed concerned for the well being of the calves. I could tell they were his prized possessions and he would give them only the best of care. After all, they were the lifeblood of his operation. Watching him that day made me realize the importance of paying attention to even the smallest details when it came to the cattle.

As we rode back to the corrals Mr. Billings explained more about owning cattle. He told me that among other things I'd have to register a brand with the state livestock board. That way I could keep track of which cows and calves were mine. He told me that once I had my brand registered we'd brand the cows and calves they'd sold me. I thought, *Sold me? They practically gave them to me.*

Listening to Mr. Billings made me understand the seriousness of the project I was about to undertake. I was a greenhorn and I knew it. I didn't realize it at the time, but that weekend would be yet another major factor that helped shape my life.

We rode into the corrals and over to the barn and unsaddled. Clay and I helped Ernesto and Diego throw out hay to the horses and then went up to the house for lunch. Ernesto and Diego went into town and visited with relatives that afternoon.

Later that day, we took it easy. Clay pulled out his guitar and played awhile. I listened as they all sang a few songs. I could tell it wasn't the first time they had sung together. They sounded pretty darn good.

It had been a pretty long day so we turned in early that night.

The next morning the three of us were off to the bus stop in Clay's hot rod pickup. I couldn't wait to get home from school that day to talk to Mom about the deal Mr. Billings and Clay had offered me. I still couldn't believe it.

Chapter Eight
Breaking The News

School seemed to drag by that day. All I could think about was telling Mom and my grandparents about the offer Mr. Billings had made me on the cows and calves. I just knew they weren't going to believe it.

I didn't want to say much to Miss Griggs about it until I had spoken to Mom, but I remembered Miss Griggs had mentioned that Mr. Billings had discussed my situation with her. Perhaps he had already told her what he was going to do.

Mom was waiting for me when school let out. I threw my duffle bag into the trunk and got in the car. "Well, how did it go?" Mom asked.

I looked at her, unable to put into words all that had happened over the weekend. It was as though I was trying to explain a wonderful dream I'd had the night before. I just stared at her. Finally I said, "Mom, Mr. Billings and Clay made me an offer that you are not going to believe!"

"Really? What was it?"

"Well, you know how I've been fretting over what to do for an agriculture project for Miss Griggs' class?"

"Yes."

"Uh, how do I put this?"

"For gosh sakes, Tyler, just tell me what's going on!"

"Well, we had gathered some cows and calves and had them penned up. Mr. Billings wanted to let them settle out a little before we started separating off the calves. He asked Clay and me to look them over with him. As we were standing there talking he presented me with an offer. He wants to give me six of their cows and calves. In turn I have to pay him half of what the calves bring when they're sold this year as payment. The cows are already bred, so next year the profits on the calves will be all mine after I pay grazing costs and expenses on the cows and calves. The only stipulation is that the money has to go into an account for college. "

"Why Tyler! That's the most generous offer I've ever heard of!"

"That's not all, Mom. Mr. Billings is going to pay me fifty dollars a day when I work at the ranch. He said that money was mine to use as I saw fit."

"We have to get home so you can explain all of this to your Granddad. He's not going to believe it!"

Mom didn't take the scenic route to Granddad's house that day. You'd have thought she was driving in a NASCAR race. I can't remember ever seeing her that excited. It almost seemed like she was more thrilled about it than I was.

Granddad was sitting in the family room watching the afternoon news on Channel Nine when we walked in. He looked up at me with a grin. "Well, I see that you survived, cowboy. Come over here and tell me about your weekend."

I walked over and sat next to him. "Granddad, it was one of the most memorable times I believe I've ever experienced. You were right when you told me that there was more to being a cowboy than wearing boots and a big hat." Then I went over the business deal that Mr. Billings and Clay had offered me.

Granddad had a strange reaction to the news. He wasn't as excited as Mom was. I believe he knew from his experiences working on ranches that there weren't any free lunches and I would earn every dime I was paid. He said, "Well, you've got your work cut out for you."

Later that evening I spent about two hours on my computer researching livestock diseases that were common in Arizona. I wanted to learn all I could about the cattle industry. I knew with the opportunity that Mr. Billings had given me I could succeed if I put my heart and soul into it. At this point in my life I knew I had to latch onto something. The only way I could prove myself was to give it all I could.

The next day before Ag class, I met with Miss Griggs. I wanted to tell her about my project plans and get her reaction. As I walked into her office she looked up. "Good afternoon, Tyler."

"Good afternoon, Miss Griggs. Ma'am, I've got some pretty interesting information to give you regarding my Ag project. This past weekend I was helping Mr. Billings and Clay brand some calves and they offered me quite a deal."

Miss Griggs smiled. "Mr. Billings told me he had something in mind for you. I just didn't know exactly what it was."

When I told her the extent of the offer she had a hard time believing it. She told me she had never heard of anyone being that generous with an FFA student. She went on to say that if I really put my heart into it and worked hard there would be no reason I would not receive the State Farmer Degree by the end of my senior year.

I hadn't thought about that. The only thing I'd been concentrating on was developing a decent Supervised Agriculture Program. Awards hadn't been a part of my life in the past. They were something Dad received for being a soldier. I never thought I was deserving of awards.

There was one prize I wanted to win though, and that was a trophy buckle. After I saw those trophy cases at the ranch with the buckles Clay and his dad had won I knew I had to win one… someday… some how.

We worked in the shop that week. I had never welded before and was glad to be introduced to it. Miss Griggs gave us basic instruction in the classroom and then we went into the shop and began working with the welding machines. Clay and I partnered up and began running beads on flat plate. Soon we were welding two pieces of metal together. I was beginning to learn things I had never dreamed I would learn.

We had a few exams in other classes that week prior to Spring Break. It was pretty intense. Clay didn't seem himself either. On Thursday, I asked him if he was feeling okay. That's when he told me his mother had been seeing a doctor in Tucson.

So that's why Ginny's been staying at home with her so much. Mrs. Billings had seemed tired when I was out there over the weekend, but she'd kept a cheerful attitude.

"What does the doctor say is wrong, Clay?" I asked.

Clay looked up. There was a mist in his eyes. "The doctor said she has a cancer. It's… it's really advanced."

"Oh my God, Clay! Is there anything we can do to help?" I asked.

"Really, Tyler… I don't know. I don't even know what I can do at this point. This was the last thing I ever expected. She's always been so healthy."

"Do you still want me to come out over Spring Break to help brand?"

"We sure do! We really need your help... even more now and especially Dad. He's fit to be tied. He doesn't sleep at night. He's just a mess. Poor Ginny is helping with Mom, plus doing the house chores and cooking for all of us and trying to get her school work done. Mom doesn't have the energy to do much of anything right now."

"Listen, Clay, your family will get through this, believe me! There are a lot of people out here who care about you and love you. We'll all be there for you."

Clay held out his hand and we shook on it.— He looked at me. "It's only been a short time, but you've become the brother I never had." He turned and walked toward the bus.

Mom was waiting for me at the usual spot. When I got in the car, she said, "What's the matter Tyler? You seem distraught."

"Guess I am Mom." I said. "You know how Mrs. Billings has been feeling poorly?"

"I knew she wasn't feeling well for sometime. Why?"

"Clay just informed me she's in the final stages of cancer."

"Oh my heavens, Tyler! When did they find

out?" She asked.

"She's been seeing a doctor in Tucson over the past year. She went up there this week for a check up and they informed her it had advanced dramatically. Clay said his dad isn't handling it well at all. He also told me they'll need me for sure for the branding. Poor Ginny will be left with all the cooking for the crew since Mrs. Billings is so sick."

"That poor girl. She does the work of a girl twice her age. She's so mature it isn't funny. I'll bet she never had a chance to just be a girl," Mom said.

We didn't say much else. We were both deep in thought. When we reached Granddad's house Mom said, "Do you think Mrs. Billings would mind if I came out and gave Ginny a hand with the cooking and house chores during the branding?"

"I don't know, Mom. I'll phone out to the ranch in awhile and ask Clay. He can ask his folks."

Later that evening I called Clay. "Hello, Clay How you doing? Glad to hear that. How's your mom? Good, I'm glad. Clay I told Mom what you told me about your mom. I also explained that Ginny would be faced with all the cooking for the crew during the branding next week. Mom was wondering if maybe she could come out and help Ginny with some of the work around the kitchen?

Okay, I'll hold on. Yeah she's sure. Okay, I'll tell her. See you tomorrow. 'Bye!" I turned to Mom. "Mom, Clay said Mrs. Billings would really appreciate it if you didn't mind. She said she knew Ginny could really use the help."

Mom had a different expression on her face when I gave her the news. It was one of wanting to help, but not knowing what was in store for her. After all she had never been on a ranch before, much less during a branding and cooking for a hungry crew of cowboys. This was going to be a new experience for her. Knowing my mom she would want to be attentive to Mrs. Billings as well. Mom was that way, a caregiver.

We decided that Friday after school Mom would drive us all out to the ranch. She would let Clay and me off at his pickup and she and Ginny would ride into the ranch together.

Chapter Nine
The Spring Break Branding

Mom met us that Friday after school and we headed out to the ranch. She let Clay and me out at his pickup and then followed us to the ranch.

Mr. Billings was there to meet us when we drove in. He walked up to Mom as she got out of her car, taking off his hat and holding out his right hand to shake her hand. "Afternoon, Mrs. Roland. It was so kind of you to volunteer to help us out this week. Norma's in the house."

"Pete," Mom said. "Please just call me Kay. I realize you men of the West are respectful of women, but I'd just like to be called Kay. It's easier for everyone."

Mr. Billings nodded, then turned to us. "Clay, you boys get Mrs. Roland's suitcase—I mean Kay's suitcase—into the house."

Clay laughed. "Okay Dad we got it."

Things went well from that time on. Mom sat and talked with Mrs. Billings for over an hour before she and Ginny began preparing supper.

Mr. Billings, Clay and I went down to the barn to take care of the evening chores.

While we were down there I looked toward the working pens and saw Ernesto and Diego throwing out hay. There must have been at least a hundred and eighty head of calves out there. We had our work cut out for us this weekend, and next week would bring even more.

That evening we sat in the family room and talked. I think Mrs. Billings wanted to learn more about Mom's background. She sure asked a lot of questions. The one that seemed to get to Mom was how she was able to cope with Dad's death. Perhaps Mrs. Billings asked that one for her husband's benefit.

He did listen quite intently to Mom as she answered that particular question. I could tell it bothered Mom but she handled it well. She must have known Mrs. Billings was trying to help her husband prepare for the inevitable.

Accepting death is difficult at best, whether it's sudden as it was for Mom and me or drawn out as it would be for the Billings family. What you do with your life is what counts. You can either give up, or move on and do something with your life.

About nine we decided we'd better hit the hay. Ginny had twin beds in her room so Mom shared the room with her. That worked out well. Clay and I wandered into his boar's nest and soon everything was quiet except for the occasional howl of a coyote. Clay called those "Prairie Hymns."

It was dark outside when we walked into the

kitchen that Saturday morning. There was Mom and Ginny whipping up our morning vittles.

Did it ever smell good! Ernesto and Diego came in and we all sat down and wolfed it down. As we got up to leave, we all thanked Mom and Ginny for the fine breakfast.

We caught our horses and saddled them at the barn, then went about preparing the branding: pot, irons, vaccines, smears and other needed equipment. Soon we were cutting off the calves and the branding was on.

Luckily that day a couple of neighbors came over to give us a hand. Clay told me they were old friends of the family. He said the two families always neighbored when it came to big brandings and shippings. He also said these two guys were tough enough to go bear hunting with a hickory switch and give the bear the switch. I found that out for myself.

For the whole next week they worked right alongside of us and never sat down for a minute unless it was for lunch. Then they each ate about a dozen *carne seca* burritos and drank a gallon of sweet tea. I'd never seen anything like it. It was good to be able to call Ben and Frank my friends.

It took us two days to brand that first bunch of calves. By the time we were finished with them we had branded one hundred eighty-seven. We'd also had to castrate seventy-five bull calves. It was a hard two days.

For the rest of the week we gathered three more pastures. Each one of them had between one hundred thirty and one hundred sixty head of cows in it. All told that week we branded six hundred sixty-four head of black baldy calves.

I learned what it meant to earn a day's wages. I'd never worked so hard in my entire life. Most people think being a cowboy is a romantic way of life. Well, in a lot of ways it is. But it's a hard life and it's filled with hard work and sometimes it can be pretty dangerous. But there's one thing for sure: it's a good life, one that most who have lived it wouldn't want to trade for anything in the world. It's a solid way to live.

Mom really came through for us that week. Not only did she take care of our meals, but she also helped Ginny care for Mrs. Billings. It seemed like Mrs. Billings was relieved to know Mom was there to make sure everything was being taken care of.

I felt so bad for Mrs. Billings. She was getting so frail. It was like she had lost ten pounds just that past week. She could hardly get around without someone helping her.

Watching Mr. Billings as Ginny or Mom helped Mrs. Billings walk was difficult. The expressions on his face cut me to the quick. His chiseled facial features would become even more pronounced and at times his eyes would fill with tears. He was such a strong man.

That week was also filled with the excitement of the upcoming 4-H bake sale and dance at the fair grounds. That was an annual event sponsored by Cochise County 4-H Clubs. Members would bring items they would prepare and they were auctioned off. Mom worked all week with Ginny experimenting with different ideas for her contribution for the 4-H bake sale. Mrs. Billings sat in the kitchen observing. Every now and then you could hear the three of them laughing about a dish or baked item that didn't quite make the grade. It was nice to know Mrs. Billings was enjoying herself. God knows she needed it.

That Saturday Ernesto and Diego had volunteered to hang around and take care of the chores and watch out for things around the ranch. There had seemed to be increased numbers of illegals moving through the area over the past month or so. It was making ranchers in the area uneasy. There had been a break-in and some rifles stolen. Mr. Billings knew that Ernesto and Diego wouldn't put up with any of that nonsense.

We piled into the Billings' suburban and headed for the fair grounds. It was getting pretty crowded when we got there. Ginny had baked a white cake with coconut icing, an apple pie and a peach cobbler. Clay and I carried all of it into the building for her while Mom and Mr. Billings helped Mrs. Billings.

I'd never been to anything like that before. I met people of all ages from all over Cochise County. They were extremely friendly. It seemed like everyone knew each other or were related in some way or another. For sure there were plenty of girls our age to look over and I wasn't related to any of 'em. That was a good thing!

When the auction finally started the auctioneer announced that whoever was top bidder on an item got to dance with the gal who baked it. That really put the boys to bidding. Some of those pies went for fifteen dollars. Ginny's cake with coconut icing went for twenty. I tried to buy it but a fella from San Simon kept outbidding me. I ended up with the peach cobbler.

I picked up the cobbler and Mom dished it out. Mr. Billings bought us vanilla ice cream to put on it. I must say that was some of the best peach cobbler I had ever tasted. Ginny sure knew what she was doing when it came to baking. Besides that I had secured a dance with her.

Country music and dancing were new to me. I had never really paid much attention to them. Back in North Carolina there were plenty of radio stations that played country, but I listened to rock most of the time.

When it came time to dance with Ginny I felt uneasy. I had never danced to country music. I must say she was a forgiving partner. I stepped on her toes so many times she laughed. "Do they do a lot of toe dancing where you come from?"

I didn't know how to answer her. I just turned red and giggled out of nervousness.

She smiled. "Don't worry, Tyler. Before too long I'll have you two steppin' like a pro."

I knew right there and then Ginny and I would be attending more dances together.

We all really enjoyed that evening. Ginny's baked goods were a big hit. It was great meeting new people who made us feel so welcome. Mom and I talked about that evening quite often after that and how much we enjoyed ourselves. It helped soften the blow of losing Dad and having to move away from what we thought was our comfort zone.

Sunday Mom and I stayed at the ranch until around six in the evening. Clay and I had done the evening chores and Mom had fixed a nice supper for everyone. Mom asked Mr. Billings if she would be needed any longer. He said no, that she'd done more than her share already and thanked her profusely.

Mom walked over to where Mrs. Billings was sitting. "Norma, if you need anything please don't hesitate to call me. I'll get out here as quickly as I can with whatever you need. I know Ginny has been staying home from school to help you. If you need someone here with you please let me know. I'd be more than happy to come out and help you."

Mrs. Billings looked at Mom, her eyes moist with tears. "Thank you so much, Katherine, for all you've done for me. I will call you. Thank you."

Mom and I gathered up our belongings and Clay helped me carry everything out to the car. Mr. Billings walked out with us. He shook Mom's hand again, then said, "Thanks again, Kay. I don't know what we'd'a done without you."

"Not a problem, Pete. I was thrilled to be able to pitch in. Remember, if Norma needs assistance call me."

Pete opened the car door for Mom.

As we drove away Pete and Clay were watching us and waving goodbye. Mom honked the horn.

Chapter Ten
Life Changes

Almost five months had gone by since that New Year's Eve when Colonel Cone and Chaplain Beeler had brought us the news about Dad. Never would I have believed my life would have taken the path it was now on. At that time I knew nothing about ranches or even cattle, much less the FFA or 4-H. My life revolved around the normal things a military dependent would do.

Meeting Clay Billings that first day at Douglas High was a godsend. He and his family had given me an entirely new perspective on life. I had learned new things, important things. My desire to work with livestock had become a central part of my life.

School also became easier to handle as time went by. I lost the insecure feelings I had that first day. Miss Griggs and my new friends in the FFA had taken me in, just as the Billings family had done. I felt a deep obligation to do the best I could for all of them. You might say it became an obsession to learn all I could in my agriculture classes.

Working at the Billings ranch only enhanced my eagerness to learn. Mr. Billings, Clay and the other cowboys became a family of mentors. Little did I realize at the time just how significant that would become.

I'll never forget the weekend at the ranch in May, just before school was about to let out for the summer. The branding was pretty much completed and things were sort'a routine. Riding fence, checking water lines and checking the cattle. We'd pick up an occasional calf we'd missed or one that had been born after the main work was done, but for the most part it was normal everyday ranch work. Even so I truly enjoyed it. Just being out on the ranch was great. There was always plenty of wildlife to watch as we rode through the pastures checking cattle.

I especially enjoyed watching new fawns as they tried to keep up with their mothers when we approached them on horseback. The rolling hills covered with Black Grama Grass and scrub oak gently rose to meet the spectacular Chiricahua Mountains, where in years past the Apaches moved freely between the Arizona Territory and Mexico.

Yes, this was a majestic country. There wasn't the thick pine forest of North Carolina or the beaches along the Atlantic Coast, but it was a country filled with magnificent scenery and a history of rugged individuals who had carved out a way of life that many only dreamed of. I thanked God every day that I had come to live that dream.

Mr. Billings and Clay sprang another surprise on me that weekend. We had been out early that Saturday morning checking water lines. As we rode along in the Jeep Mr. Billings said, "Tyler, how would you like to start learning to team rope?"

I was in a state of shock. I had begun learning to handle a rope a little from almost the first weekend I was at the ranch. Clay helped me get the hang of it when he was practicing on his mechanical roping machine. I'd catch now and then, but there was no way I was at the same level as Clay and for sure not Mr. Billings. They were really accomplished ropers. Now they'd asked me if I wanted to get serious about roping.

Mr. Billings said, "Clay and I have talked it over this past week and came to the conclusion it was time you practiced in the arena with us. I picked up twenty-five head of Corrientes last week from Dan Stradling over in Nogales. They're ready to start roping."

Clay chimed in. "What do you say, Tyler? When schools out we're gonna start hittin' some rodeos and team ropin's. Dad and I thought you might want to tag along."

I must have looked like the cat had my tongue. I couldn't believe what I had just heard. "Would I ever!" I blurted out. "I'd love to learn!"

"Then it's settled," Mr. Billings said. "When we

get back, we'll bring those steers in from the trap and get started. Ernesto and Diego can work the roping chute for us."

Clay said, "We'll have to run it for them a couple of times Dad. You know how they like to rope!"

"Yeah, that's for sure," Mr. Billings said. "Those two are ropers for sure. I've seen them win some pretty good ropin's. That trophy saddle Ernesto just won is a testament to that fact."

Clay said, "Not to mention the buckles they've won. I'll bet each of 'em have at least six."

Not one time did Mr. Billings or Clay mention that each of them had a trophy saddle or two and a display case full of trophy buckles. They could only sing the praises of their two friends, Ernesto and Diego.

As we rode along in the Jeep all I could think of was maybe someday I'd be a good enough roper to win a buckle. When we reached the barn, Mr. Billings said, "Tyler, you saddle up Nubbin. He's a well-seasoned heeling horse and he'll give you an honest shot every time."

Mr. Billings was not only giving me the chance to start learning to team rope, he was letting me use one of the best roping horses he had. Nubbin was the horse he'd ridden when he won most of the buckles I'd seen in his case. What an honor it was to saddle that beautiful black gelding.

Soon we had the steers gathered and in the crowding pen behind the roping chute. Ernesto and Diego began running the steers into the chute and putting on the horn wraps.

Mr. Billings called me over and began to explain what I needed to be paying attention to when I roped. He explained where I should be when the header set and turned the steer and how I should handle the rope. He then said, "For God's sake, Tyler, keep your thumb up when you dally and your hand out of the coils. We don't want to lose any thumbs or fingers today."

I took what he was saying to heart. I'd already seen a couple of ropers with stubs where their thumb and fingers had been before they got hung up dallying. I wanted no part of that action. Clay had shown me how to hold the rope and keep my digits out of the coils when we were practicing on the roping dummy. I felt confident that I could manage the dallying okay.

We had warmed up the horses and Mr. Billings called out, "Clay, go ahead and head one for Tyler."

"Okay, Dad," Clay hollered back.

We headed for the chute where a Corriente steer seemed to be waiting, not knowing what was in store for him. Clay headed for the header's box and I turned Nubbin around and backed into the corner of the heeler's box.

Like Mr. Billings said, he was seasoned. As soon as I backed him into the box, he knew what he was there for. His ears pointed and he gathered himself beneath me like a tightly wound watch, ready to spring into action. I knew he'd do his job. Could I do mine?

"You ready?" Clay said.

My mouth was dry, and my insides were trembling with both fear and excitement. I was about to make my first run at a steer. Who would have ever believed Tyler Roland would be sitting on a $25,000 heeling horse about to try to catch a 500 pound steer by two hind legs? I knew right then and there the adrenaline rush I was feeling would be with me the rest of my life. I looked over at Clay and nodded.

Clay looked at Ernesto and nodded. Ernesto pulled the lever on the roping chute. The doors sprang open and the steer bolted into the arena.

Clay had position on him in four strides and roped him clean around the horns. He set the steer perfectly and turned off to the left at an even pace.

Nubbin seemed to be watching the steer as he turned, because without much from me he turned and put me in perfect position for a throw at the heels. I was so nervous that when I threw my rope the loop just bounced off the side of the steer and fell empty on the ground as Clay rode away, pulling the steer behind him.

He stopped and turned toward me. "That wasn't too awful bad for your first time." He chuckled. "At least you hit 'im in the side." Clay then followed the steer down to the stripping chute while I rode back to where Mr. Billings was standing.

"Not bad, Tyler." Mr. Billings said. "When you bring up your arm to swing the rope, try to get your elbow up a little more and swing the loop so that it will dip a little right over the middle of the steer's back. When you swing the rope bring the loop under the steer as he brings his legs back and release it. When the steer brings his legs forward he'll probably run them right into your open loop. All you need to do then is set your horse as you pull some slack and go to the horn. It takes awhile to start getting timed up with the steer, but the more runs you make the better you'll get at it. It's like anything you do in sports; it takes plenty of practice to get good at it. One last thing —when you practice, practice like you're sitting first in the short go, the check is on the line and you haven't eaten in two days. Be serious with your practice!"

Clay rode up to us. "Ready for another one, Tyler?"

"You bet." As I rode toward the heeler's box. I was trying to digest everything Mr. Billings had said. I backed Nubbin into the corner of the box.

Again Clay looked over at me. "You ready?"

"Yep," I replied.

Clay nodded at Ernesto and another steer sprang into the arena at a run.

Again Clay's horse Woodrow had put him in position in just a few strides. Again Clay made a clean catch around the steer's horns, set him and turned off.

Nubbin was right there again, in perfect position for a heel loop. My mind was racing a hundred miles per hour. *Get your elbow up... dip the tip of your loop over the steer's back... watch the steer's back legs... time up...time up*, I thought as I dipped the loop just over the steer's back. I released the rope just as the steer's legs started back. As the legs came forward they were in my loop. Nubbin set up like the pro he was and I dallied.

Clay spun Woodrow around as he felt the steer come to an abrupt stop. He looked at me and yelled, "All right, Tyler! Great run!"

Mr. Billings and the two cowboys were yelling praises as I rode back to the chute. *I did it!* I thought. *I caught my first steer in an arena!* It wasn't for a buckle or a big check, but I still felt ten feet tall and bullet proof. I had done something else I never believed I would do.

As I rode up to where Mr. Billings was standing, he looked up at me with a smile. "Tyler, you keep that up and you'll be cashing checks in no time. That was a fine run. Especially seeing how it was only your second time out of a heeler's box. Looks like we have a natural on our hands."

Clay rode up. "Looks like I have a knew roping partner for the high school rodeos this summer. That was all right, Tyler."

"I think I'll need a lot more practice to get consistent."

"Yeah," Clay said. "But you're in the right place to get it. We'll stay at it, then hit a couple of small ropings in a month or so. You'll be ready to get your feet wet by then. Who knows? Maybe next year we'll qualify for the National High School Championship Rodeo."

I laughed. "Well, that might be pushing it a little. I've got a lot to learn."

Mr. Billings shook his head. "Clay's right. You keep practicing and improving on runs like that and you'll be hard to beat at high school rodeos. You and Clay could make a good team."

With that all said I decided to loosen Nubbin's chinch and give him a breather. I tied him to the arena fence and went over and started loading the chute for Ernesto and Diego. They alternated with Mr. Billings while Clay and I kept the steers loaded. It was a real lesson watching the two cowboys and Mr. Billings rope. They made it all look so easy. I understood what Mr. Billings meant when he told me to always practice like it was for the check. That's just how the three of them practiced.

I'll never forget that day as long as I live. Roping became an important part of my life and would eventually help me get a college education. The friendships I was making and would develop in the future would change my life forever.

Chapter Eleven
Mrs. Billings

Even though everything seemed peaceful around the ranch, something had taken the sense of normalcy away. Pete was very troubled and seemed to be depressed a great deal of the time.

The trips to Tucson for Mrs. Billing's doctor appointments were becoming more frequent. Mr. Billings became less talkative and didn't leave the house much. It was like he was afraid to be away from Mrs. Billings.

She was losing weight and becoming frail and unable to do her normal work around the house. Pete began helping Ginny more with the household chores and when Ginny and Clay were at school Pete left the ranch work to Ernesto and Diego.

Mr. and Mrs. Billings had returned home late Friday night from one of the trips to Tucson. The next morning, Mr. Billings told us that he and Mrs. Billings would like to have a little meeting with us after breakfast.

Mrs. Billings wasn't at breakfast. When we had finished eating Mr. Billings asked us to come into the living room. Ginny, Clay and I walked into the room. Mrs. Billings was sitting silently in her favorite rocking chair. She looked frail. Her face was pale and her eyes had lost the glow of the happy, energetic lady I had known.

I got a sinking feeling, and it brought back memories of the night Chaplain Beeler and Colonel Cone came to the house to inform Mom and me about Dad.

When we'd all sat down, Pete said, "Kids...." He cleared his throat. "As you know the trips to Tucson have become more frequent over the last month." He paused and looked at Clay and Ginny. His eyes began to grow moist and he wiped a tear from his cheek with his strong, calloused hand. Then he began again. "This is pretty tough."

With a soft, weak voice Mrs. Billings said, "Go ahead Pete... you're doing fine."

He looked up at us again. "Well, y'see... Norma has been going through some extremely rough times with her illness. The Chemo Therapy hasn't been able to stop the cancer from spreading. Yesterday, her doctor informed us that she's in stage four of the cancer. It seems there's not much that they can do for her."

Ginny began to sob and ran over to hug her mother. Clay looked across the room at me, his eyes filling with tears. Then he looked at his dad. "What do you mean there's nothing they can do for her?" He wiped his eyes. "Surely there must be something!"

"Son, I thought the same thing when Doctor Grayem told us. He assured us they would do all that was possible... but the prognosis didn't look all that favorable."

I tried to console Clay the best I could. My insides felt like they had been ripped out for the second time in less than a year. I had to be there for this fine family, just as they had been for me when my ordeal had brought me to Arizona.

Clay looked at his dad. "What are we supposed to do Dad? I mean, how can we help Mom?"

Mrs. Billings smiled weakly.

Pete said, "We just have to be strong for her." He looked at his wife, then back to Clay. "We have to make sure she has everything possible to comfort her through this journey."

No one said a thing. You could have heard a pin drop.

Again the strength of this fine man had manifested itself. It was difficult for me as I watched the three of them with her. It was just surreal.

Tears were streaming down Mrs. Billings' cheeks. With a trembling voice she said, "I'll do all I can to get through this. But I want you all to know I'm ready for whatever God has in store for me. I love you all very much." She then looked over at me. "Tyler... you've become my second son. I want you to know I love you."

I was trying to hold back my tears, trying to be strong for my wonderful friends, but when she said that, I couldn't hold back anymore.

Mrs. Billings looked at her husband. "Pete... would you help me back to the bedroom so I can rest please?"

He gently helped her stand and slowly walked her to her room. Clay and Ginny watched as their mother walked away.

Clay looked at me. "What do we do now, Tyler?"

"Clay, Ginny... you're going to have to draw on strength you never knew you had. Your dad's going to need all the help you can possibly give him now. It's not gonna be easy." I thought for a moment, then said. "Maybe we should saddle up and just take a little ride. It might help us clear our minds. It's like some old guy once said: There's nothing better for the inside of a man than the outside of a horse."

"Maybe you're right Tyler," Clay said. "Maybe we should just ride out a ways."

Ginny looked at us. "Would you boys mind if I tagged along?"

Immediately, Clay said, "No problem, Sis... you're more than welcome."

Clay went in and told his dad and mom we were going to take a little horseback ride.

That was one of the longest weekends of my life. It seemed like we were all in a state of shock. We went about our normal chores but we all seemed to be in a cloud. Mr. Billings hardly left his wife's bedside. Clay and I tried to practice our roping, but just couldn't seem to get into it. Ginny did a lot of cooking for us. She prepared some pretty decent meals and her baking skills seemed to be improving.

When I got home that Monday, I told Mom about Mrs. Billings. She seemed like she already knew. She looked at me. "Tyler, I was afraid of this. They've had to go to Tucson quite a bit lately. I thought the doctors were probably trying everything possible. The last time I was at the ranch Norma told me it wasn't going well. It was like she had begun to prepare herself for what she thought was the inevitable."

"You mean she already knew?"

She nodded. "I'm afraid so. I think a person just knows when she's not going to get well. Her cancer was spreading despite the chemo."

"What can we do to help them?"

"I'm not sure. I'll have to think on that a little." Not saying another word, she walked out of the room.

That evening at supper Mom broke the news to my grandparents. My grandmother couldn't believe it. She just kept saying over and over, "That poor family... that poor family."

The next day I was waiting for Clay's bus to arrive. When he got off, I walked over to him. "Morning, Clay. How are you doing today?"

"Oh... pretty good. Ginny stayed home though. She wanted to do some laundry and straighten up around the house. She said she had to make sure Mom had plenty to eat."

"That's Ginny all right. She's quite a gal. I just hope her schooling doesn't get behind with her staying home so much."

"That's got Dad and me concerned too." Clay said. "Ginny's just afraid when Dad's out working Mom might need some help... she's so weak. The medications are causing her problems. She doesn't seem to be able to hold anything down."

"Does your Dad have any ideas on what to do?"

"Dad thinks we need to have someone to stay with her. That way Ginny won't be missing so much school." Clay paused. "Tyler... did your mom find a job yet?"

"No... not yet." I realized what he was thinking. "And that might be a perfect fit! After all, Mom and your mom got to know each other and got along well. Have you talked it over with your dad yet?"

"No... Actually I just thought about it.

I'll talk to him tonight and let you know what he says tomorrow."

Clay and I went through our morning classes, then met up at the Ag room. Miss. Griggs had us working on our record keeping, trying to get everything in order before the end of the year.

It took me the entire period to work up my business plan for my cows that Mr. Billings was selling me. I also did some entries regarding the work I'd been doing at the ranch. My Supervised Agricultural Experience Program was taking shape. It surprised me as to how much work I'd done over the last couple of months. When I read over my entries, I was determined to do even more over the next year.

Before Clay got back on the bus that day we agreed on the plan we'd made regarding Mom helping Mrs. Billings.

That evening I approached Mom about it. "Mom, could I talk with you about something?"

"Sure, Tyler. "

"Well, Ginny's been missing a lot of school. She's been staying home helping her Mom. Mr. Billings has been talking about maybe hiring someone to stay with her. Clay and I discussed the situation and we thought... well, since you haven't found a job yet, maybe you could stay with his mom. That way Ginny wouldn't be missing so much school."

Mom looked a bit surprised at the idea. "What do Mr. and Mrs. Billings have to say about this idea?"

"Clay's going to talk with them tonight about it."

"I'll have to think on that a little." Mom said. "Besides, we don't know what Clay's folks are going to say about it."

"Would you think on it though?" I asked.

"Yes, I'll think about it. There's just a lot to consider. I'd almost have to live at the ranch in order to look after her like that. I couldn't drive out there everyday from town."

"I'll let Clay know in the morning."

When the bus arrived the next morning, Clay got off but still no Ginny.

"Hey Clay. How'd things go with your folks?"

"Well, Ginny and I and Dad discussed it at length. Dad's going to call your mom later today and talk with her." His eyes welling with tears, he shrugged. "We all know something has to be done. Ginny can't continue to miss school."

When I got home that afternoon Mom informed me that she had spoken with Mr. Billings about the situation and they had come to an agreement. Mom would take some things to the ranch the next weekend and begin staying with Mrs. Billings. It was uncertain how long Mom would be needed, but Mrs. Billings would receive the best care possible.

Chapter Twelve
Friendship

It's a funny thing about friendships and what leads to them. Some people grow up having best friends in the early stages of life, and sometimes those friends grow distant as their lives progress. For Mom and Mrs. Billings a true friendship came about later in life. It was a friendship forged out of a devastating event in Afghanistan and a terrible disease called lung cancer. It was a friendship like many hear about but never experience... a true friendship.

I'll never forget the first weekend that Mom went to the ranch to care for Mrs. Billings. She had spent the prior week studying all she could about lung cancer and how it affected women. Mom just couldn't understand how Mrs. Billings came down it. Lung cancer was thought to be a man's disease caused by smoking.

Prior to researching the disease, Mom didn't realize it caused more deaths in women than breast and uterine cancer combined. Many women who had lung cancer were life-long non-smokers, just as Mrs. Billings was. Mom couldn't believe Mrs. Billings was one of those unfortunate women. She made up her mind to do all she could for her.

Friday after school Mom picked Clay and me up. We drove out to the ranch, let Clay off at his usual parking spot, then followed him to the ranch.

When we arrived at the house, Mr. Billings walked out to meet us. He looked gaunt and tired, as though he hadn't slept or eaten all week. It was obvious he was worried beyond words. As we got out of the car he said, "It's so good to see you again, Mrs. Roland. Thank you so much for coming."

Mom smiled. "Pete, remember, it's Kay, not Mrs. Roland."

Pete smiled, probably for the first time in days. "Thanks for reminding me, Kay. I plumb forgot. I guess I'm just not myself these days."

"Bless your heart," Mom said. "Maybe I can take some of the load off your and Ginny's shoulders. You both need some relief from your worries, that's for sure."

Clay and I took Mom's bags from the car and we all went into the house. Ginny was sitting next to her mother. She looked like an angel comforting her. The responsibility she had taken upon herself had matured her beyond her years.

Mom walked over and knelt down beside Mrs. Billings. "Hello Norma. How are you today?"

Mrs. Billings looked at her with a labored smile. "Oh... all right I guess. Don't think I could cook for a branding crew right now… but I'll make it I think."

Mom gave her a hug. "That's what I'm here for. I can do the cooking. You just rest."

Ginny looked over at Mom. "Thank you so much for coming out, Mrs. Roland. We can sure use the help."

Mom got the strangest look on her face. Almost like she was fighting back tears. She smiled at Ginny. "Young lady you've been a real big help to your mom. It's time you take a break and let me do some of the work around here. You need to start concentrating on your schooling again. I'll be here for your mom. Rest assured I'll do everything in my power to see to her every need."

Ginny threw her arms around Mom. "Thank you so much, Mrs. Roland."

I'll never forget watching the three of them. It was like watching three women bonding in a way only they could understand. These were extreme circumstances. Each of them knew they would have to see the journey through no matter how difficult it would become.

Mr. Billings looked at Clay and me. "Well boys, we'd better get down to the barn and get some chores done."

The three of us walked toward the barn, not saying a thing. Finally Clay cleared his throat." Tyler… how did you prepare for your father's death?"

Mr. Billings looked at him, startled. "Clay, that's no kind of question to be asking Tyler!"

"That's okay, Mr. Billings," I said. "It's like this, Clay... I... I didn't have time to prepare for it. When Colonel Cone and Chaplain Beeler came to the house early that morning, Mom and I were welcoming in a new year. We were looking forward to Dad coming home from Afghanistan in just a couple of months. He was on his second deployment and had been there nearly ten months. When they told us we must have both gone into shock."

Clay nodded. "I can't imagine what you must have gone through getting hit with that. Dad and I have talked over our situation with Mom. We both have known for a couple of years that this disease was probably going to take her from us, but...." Clay was having difficulty talking. "I... I just can't bring myself to believe Mom isn't going to be with us anymore." Tears began to stream from his eyes. "I just can't believe this is happening to us."

Mr. Billings was unable to speak. He looked straight ahead as we neared the barn., then left us and walked directly to where the two saddle horses were standing in their stalls waiting for their evening feeding.

Clay and I stopped. "Clay, I know this is a

tough time for you... maybe the toughest thing you'll ever have to go through. I just want you to know I'll be here for you and your family no matter what happens. You've become a second family to me. I never knew people could be so kind. It's my turn now. I'm here for you, brother."

"Thanks, Tyler. I know fate brought us together for a reason. We must have many good times ahead of us... I'm sure."

"You can take that to the bank." Then I tried to take his mind off things. "Besides, you still have to make a team roper out of me. We have a lot of good ropin's to get to. I can hear the announcer saying, 'Next team out is Clay Billings on the head and Tyler Roland on the heels. Watch 'em, folks! They're tough!'"

Clay looked at me and chuckled for the first time in awhile. "That's for sure, Tyler. We're gonna show 'em what team ropin's all about."

When we finished up our chores and met up with Mr. Billings, the day was coming to a close. The sun was setting over the hills west of the ranch and a yellow glow was piercing through the oak trees. In the distance a covey of Gambel's Quail were talking to each other. A slight breeze was blowing out of the south, bringing a slight hint of a rain shower.

The three of us walked toward the house in deep anticipation of what Mom and Ginny had prepared for supper. As we walked into the house we were surprised to see Mom had just prepared a pan of red chili beef enchiladas with re-fried beans. Wow what a surprise. She motioned toward the bathroom. "You boys get washed up for supper."

There was no hesitation at all. In just a few minutes we had all sat down at the table. Mom looked at Mr. Billings. "Pete, would you be so kind as to give us a blessing?"

Pete looked surprised at the request. "Why, yes... I'd be glad to." We all held hands around the old oak table. "Lord, thank you for this fine meal that has been prepared for us. I ask that it will strengthen our bodies. Above all Lord, thank you for bringing Katherine and Tyler into our lives. They are the kindest of people and truly the finest of friends. Amen."

As I recalled those times I realized a significant change had begun to emerge in all of our lives. Mom and I had already lost Dad, and our new friends were facing a challenge of their own.

The Billings family had begun to change. No longer were they as happy as they had been when I first visited the ranch. A more solemn mood had overtaken the once secure family.

Clay would sometimes question me as to how I handled the loss of my father. He was trying to adjust to the fact that he was going to lose his mother to a dreaded disease. Trying to comfort someone experiencing what he was going through wasn't easy. I felt only pain for him. I did know I had to be there for him, his sister and his father. After all they had taken me in as one of their own during some extremely dark days in my life. Now it was my turn to step up and be as good a friend as they had been to me.

Mom seemed tireless in her new calling. She kept things going around the house while at the same time helping Mrs. Billings. They would sit and talk for what seemed like hours, mostly about the more enjoyable times in their lives. Sometimes we even heard laughter coming from Mrs. Billing's room, followed by whispers. It was like she was trying to tell Mom all she could about her family.

When Mrs. Billings would finally fall asleep, Mom would sit next to her and make sure she was okay. She would then quietly leave the room and find another household chore to complete. It was as though she was trying to take her mind off of Mrs. Billings and the physical and emotional pain she was going through.

It was plain to see Mom was experiencing a very emotional time as well. She had become quite a nurse, but it was taking its toll on her. I was proud of her. She was selfless in her care for her new friend. What a wonderful friendship.

Chapter Thirteen
Practice, Practice, Practice

As time passed things began to settle into a normal routine around the ranch, or as normal as could be expected. Mom was staying there through the week, and she was adapting to ranch life very well.

Mr. Billings was able to return to his normal ranch work with Ernesto and Diego, knowing his beloved wife Norma was in good hands. He almost seemed like the Mr. Billings I had first come to know.

Clay, Ginny and I helped around the ranch after school and on the weekends. The big thing was that Ginny could now return to school on a regular basis. Her teachers were understanding and helped her catch up on much of the work she had missed.

Clay and I continued to work hard in school, but it seemed like we never were the type of student Ginny was. She excelled in all her classes and FFA activities. In fact she helped Clay and me a great deal with our project record keeping. She seemed to be a natural at accounting and entering pertinent data into the computer. Clay and I seemed to do better with the hands-on work at the ranch. When Mr. Billings saw how we were working together as a team he was very pleased.

As the year progressed I was becoming more comfortable in my new environment. Thanks to Mr. Billings and Clay my FFA projects were doing well. Miss Griggs seemed pleased with my achievements and encouraged me to continue to work harder. Her encouragement meant a great deal to me and made me want to succeed even more.

The days were getting longer and we had more time to practice our team roping when we got back to the ranch after school. Mr. Billings had asked Ernesto and Diego to keep a few head of Corrientes in the trap next to the arena so we could start practicing as soon as we got home. They were happy to do so since they knew they too would get to make a couple of runs.

Mr. Billings would always be there to coach us. We couldn't have asked for a better coach. After all he and one of his neighbors had qualified for the National Finals in years past. He seemed to want Clay and me to take his place in the arena. I learned later that it wasn't just the rodeo arena he wanted us to take his place in. He wanted us to take his place on the ranch when the time came. Mrs. Billings' condition made him realize he was not immortal. His time would also come, and he wanted us to be there when it did.

Clay and I practiced whenever possible after

school and on the weekends. The school year was drawing to an end so this meant there would be ropings and rodeos to get to. I could hardly wait to test my newfound skills at team roping, but for now Mr. Billings evaluated every run we made. When we messed up he was tough and stern with his comments. We knew he was right and that he was only doing it to improve our technique.

Clay and I were getting pretty good as a team. In time he could consistently turn steers in the seven hole and I was improving on the heels. It was getting to where I could catch eight out of ten by two feet. Still Mr. Billings insisted we continue to practice. "Practice like you're roping for a million dollars. Make every loop count."

Eventually we got to the point that he was satisfied we wouldn't be wasting our money at the ropings. One day toward the end of May he said, "Boys, there's going to be a good jackpot over in Sonoita this next weekend. Maybe we should take it in. What do you think?"

Clay and I looked at each other like it was a dream come true. Now we would see whether we could stack up against some pretty tough ropers. Clay got a serious expression on his face. "Dad, do you think Mom would be well enough to ride over and watch us?"

"Clay, I... we'll sure find out. I'm sure Kay wouldn't mind going as well. After all this will be

Tyler's first competition. I'm sure she'd love to be there."

I said, "Maybe my grandparents would like to drive over also."

"Good idea," Mr. Billings said. "We'll make a day of it. Ernesto and Diego would like to enter too, I'm sure. Let's go up to the house and talk it over with the ladies."

We all sat in the living room discussing the possibility of going to the Sonoita roping. Mom was thrilled. She looked at Mrs. Billings. "What do you think, Norma? Are you up to a trip over to Sonoita to watch our boys rope?"

Norma looked at us with a smile on her thin face. "I'd love to. I never thought I'd be able to watch a roping again. I miss the days when Pete and Clay were roping together. Now I'll be able to watch Pete rope with two of his boys."

"Well, I guess it's a done deal," Mr. Billings said. "Tyler, you'd better ask your grandparents if they'd like to tag along with us."

"I will, Sir. I'm sure Granddad will be especially glad to watch us. He's been asking me how we've been doing with our practicing. Now he'll be able to judge it for himself."

"I'm sure he won't be disappointed," Mr. Billings said.

That week seemed to just drag by. We

practiced roping every day after school and then studied for upcoming finals. We seemed to be extra busy. I often wondered whether Mr. Billings knew how tough it would be for us to prepare for the roping while studying for our finals. Maybe it was his way of testing our resolve to do well at both.

It must have worked. Clay and I did well on the finals we took that week, and that weekend in Sonoita went pretty well too. We didn't win any of the ropings, but we did manage to take Second in a three-steer average. My grandparents enjoyed the day too, and it was obvious that Mrs. Billings and Mom were thrilled to be there.

Another bright point of the day was that Ernesto and Diego won a three-steer. They roped three head in twenty-one point five seconds. It was a good payday for them.

After the roping we all went to dinner at a local steak house. The steaks were great and a band was playing some fine country music. They called themselves The Dynamite Hicks. Butch was the lead singer and there were a couple of gals that could sing lead as well as back-up. We all enjoyed our time eating good steaks, listening to country music and dancing a little. For the first time I had Ginny all to myself and we danced up a storm.

On the way back to the ranch Mr. Billings told Clay and me that he thought we did pretty well for our first time out. He told us that it was only a start, that if we continued to improve, he'd make sure we got to more ropings during the summer. Clay and I were thrilled. It looked like our practicing had begun to pay off.

That following week was very busy for our FFA Chapter. At our meeting we elected chapter officers for the next year. Clay was elected Chapter President for his senior year. With Ginny's excellent record-keeping abilities it wasn't hard to guess who would be elected Chapter Secretary, and I was elected Chapter Reporter. I was thrilled that the members would think enough of me to elect me to a chapter office. It was my first time to be elected to any sort of office. Needless to say I was really looking forward to the next year. Clay, Ginny and I would be wearing the famous blue and gold FFA jacket with our names and newly elected office on it. It was hard for me to believe I could be so lucky.

The next weekend the chapter held the annual parent-member banquet. New chapter officers were presented to the parents, guests and members. A number of awards were presented too, as well as scholarships to senior class members.

Being in the financial shape Mom and I were in after losing Dad made me realize how fortunate those who had received the scholarships were. It made me want to try even harder. Hopefully I might be lucky enough to receive one next year. There was one thing for sure: the FFA offered many opportunities for those who were motivated to achieve all they possibly could. Watching our members receive those scholarships added one more item to my list of things to do.

It was a memorable evening for me. I was glad that all of us could be there together. Even my grandparents attended. That evening Granddad took me aside and told me how proud he was of what I was doing. Then he winked and grinned. "I have some things in mind that I'll tell you about later."

Clay and I continued to practice our roping and check cattle. We fixed broken water lines weekly. The toughest chore was oiling and repairing those blasted windmills. It seemed there was always one that had to be worked on.

We went to a lot of ropings that summer, and even made a couple of trips over to New Mexico. There were some pretty tough ropers over there. It was a funny thing though: we all seemed to get along well, but when it came to rope, everyone roped to win. All of us were hungry for a win and everyone roped like it. I knew for certain if I was going to be any good roping I'd have to continue practicing every chance I got. It was a tough game.

Mom and I drove into town one Saturday to shop for groceries. She told me Granddad wanted to see us. When we arrived at his house he was putting some things in his pickup. He walked over to Mom and me. "Kay, would you mind if Tyler drove up to Tucson with me today?"

Mom gave him a strange look. "We were going to do our grocery shopping today."

"I know, Honey... but this is sort'a important to me."

"Well okay," she said. "I guess so. But he's going to have to get back to the ranch in the morning. Can you bring him out?"

"I'll make sure he gets out there," Granddad said.

Mom went in to see Grandma, and Granddad and I headed to Tucson. All the way, Granddad kept talking about his days working on ranches and doing a little rodeoing. I could tell he had enjoyed that time in his life. He kept telling me over and over how proud he was of me for taking the high road after losing my dad.

When we reached Tucson he drove directly to a Dodge dealership. I looked at him—then asked. "What are you going to do here, Granddad?"

"I have to get this truck serviced," he said. "It

needs a good going over."

After the shop manager took it back to the garage area, Granddad and I walked over to where the new pickups were on display.

"There are some nice pickups here," I said.

"Sure enough," he said.

About that time a salesman walked up. "What can I do for you today?"

Granddad looked at him. "What do you have in a one ton?"

The salesman pulled out an inventory sheet and looked it over. "I have two. One is a deluxe extended cab model and the other is a standard cab. The extended cab has a Cummings Diesel in it. It's pretty well loaded."

"Let's take a look at it," Granddad said.

"It's right down here, Sir," the salesman said. We followed him over to where a new tan pickup was sitting. "This it." He opened the driver's side door.

Granddad looked inside the open door. "Looks pretty nice."

"This is a good one," the salesman said. "It's got all the bells and whistles. Even has a towing package. We put a gooseneck hitch in it for the person who ordered it."

"Why didn't he take it?" Granddad asked.

"I'm not really sure." The salesman said. "All I know is after it was set up he couldn't take it. I'm sure the boss would treat you right on this one. The new models will be out in a month and he wants to clear out as much of the inventory as possible."

"Let's put a pencil to it," Granddad said.

As we walked toward the sales office I kept wondering why Granddad wanted another pickup. The one he had was only a couple of years old. It still had the new car smell.

After a lot of dickering and conferences with the dealership owner and the salesman, they reached a price.

Granddad looked at me. "What do you think Tyler?"

"It looks great to me, Granddad... but why do you need two pickups?"

He grinned. "Remember at the banquet I told you I had something to tell you about?"

I nodded. "Yes, I remember."

"Well, this is it. That pickup is yours."

"*What?*" I said. "Do you mean that?"

He grinned even broader. "I'm as serious as a hen laying. I didn't get a chance to help your mom like I wanted to. She married your dad, then followed him all over the world. When she called me that night she found out about your dad, I was heartsick for her. When she agreed to move out to Douglas, I made up my mind to do all I could to help you get a good start.

"Thank God you hooked up with the Billings family. I saw what Pete was doing for you and I wanted to do something too. After that first roping in Sonoita, I knew it wouldn't be your last. You'd need a good pickup to get you and Clay down the road. This pickup was just what I had in mind. And when we get back to Douglas there's something else I want to show you."

I was in a state of shock. "Granddad... I don't know what to say. I can't believe this is happening. What can I do to repay you?"

He shook his head. "Tyler, all I want is for you to continue on the path you've taken. You have a lot of potential. You've got a good mind and you know how to use it to do positive things. Just follow your heart and strive to achieve all you possibly can in life. You were dealt a bad hand when you lost your dad like that. Just put your heart into everything you do, just like he did."

I couldn't help myself. My eyes began to well up and my throat tightened. I had never heard Granddad say anything like that about Dad. For some reason I felt he disapproved of him for taking Mom away from him and Grandmother. It made me feel good to know he respected Dad for being the outstanding soldier that he was.

When Granddad's pickup was ready I followed him out of Tucson. There I was, sitting in a brand new Dodge pickup driving down I-10—*my* Dodge pickup. *It doesn't get any better than this*, I thought.

When we arrived at Granddad's house we parked and went into the house. He left the room, and when he came back he said, "Come on, Tyler. We've got one more thing to do." As we walked out he said. "We need to take your pickup."

He directed me as we drove to the other side of town. Finally he said, "Pull in here."

I drove into a lot where about four horse trailers were on display. A short, heavy-set man walked out of the sales office. "Good evening, Mr. Sanders," he said.

"Good afternoon, Jake," Granddad replied. "Do you have that trailer ready?"

"Sure do, Sir. It's right over here."

I followed them over to where a like-new three-horse slant with living quarters was parked.

"Here it is," the salesman said. "This one is like new. We only used it as a demonstrator at equestrian events. We even put new tires on it for you."

Granddad looked at me. "What do you say, Tyler? Think it will do for awhile?"

"You're joking!" I said. "First the pickup, and now *this*? I can't believe this is all happening!"

Granddad laughed. "Well, it is." He then looked at Jake. "Are we even on this?"

"Sure are, Mr. Sanders. Let me put the plate on it and get you the title."

Granddad asked, "Did you title it to Tyler Roland?"

"Sure did, Mr. Sanders."

Again I was in a state of shock. I kept waiting for Mom to wake me up for school.

We hooked up the trailer and drove up to Granddad's house.

"Tyler, I think you'd better stay here tonight and head back to the ranch in

the morning," he said.

"I think you're right, Granddad. I don't think I could make the drive tonight. Too much has gone on today. I need time to settle out."

Grandmother had prepared a nice meatloaf for dinner with mashed potatoes and corn. We sat around the table talking about the goings on around town. After supper I helped Grandmother with the dishes and then we all watched TV for a while.

Right after breakfast the next morning I headed for the ranch. When I got there everyone came out to look at my new pickup and trailer. Mr. Billings and Clay came over to where I parked. "Wow! This is quite a rig!" Mr. Billings said.

"It sure is!" Clay said as he walked around, examining it.

"Granddad bought it for me yesterday," I said.

"He told me he had something like this in mind," Pete said. "I didn't realize it was going to be like this though. This is a real going down the road rig."

"I just hope we can all put it to good use," I replied. "There's plenty of room for all of us when we head to a roping."

When school ended, Clay and I worked steadily with Mr. Billings and the two ranch hands. Everyday there was something to keep us busy. When we had time we'd take some Corriente steers to the practice pen. Some times we'd make ten to twelve runs. Our practice was beginning to pay off at the ropings. We were picking up some pretty good checks. "

Chapter Fourteen
Disappointment

Even though Clay and I were making progress with our roping, there was a dark cloud that wouldn't go away. Mrs. Billings seemed to be getting weaker.

Mom and Ginny brought her to ropings that didn't require a lot of travel and it seemed to improve her spirit, but she tired easily and they would take her back to the ranch. She always tried to be there for Clay and me, but it became more and more difficult for her.

It was obvious that it was taking a toll on Clay, too. When they would leave a roping Clay wasn't able to concentrate. In fact he became extremely withdrawn and it was difficult to get so much as a word out of him.

As he watched his mother go through the physical and emotional pain it was almost more than he could bear. It was difficult to see what this terrible disease was doing to such a fine family, a family I had grown to love as my own.

It was also hard for me to understand how Mom could be so calm. She seemed to take everything in stride. When Mrs. Billings was having an extra difficult day, Mom was there for her. When there were meals to prepare Mom always made something delicious. Mom and I didn't have a lot of time together during that time. When we did, we talked about Dad and Mrs. Billings and the work we were doing around the ranch.

On one of those occasions I asked, "Mom, how do you do it? I mean you seem to hold in your emotions so well."

She looked at me, then quietly said, "Tyler, after we lost your dad I thought my life had lost all purpose. I'd lost my one true love. And don't get me wrong—I surely loved you—but your dad was my soul mate.

"Being able to help this fine family brought new purpose into my life. I just knew I had to be strong no matter how hard it got. These folks needed our help probably more than they ever needed any help any other time in their lives. We both have to encourage them and be there for them."

A tear ran down her cheek as she stood up. "I have a roast in the oven... I'd better check."

As she walked toward the kitchen she wiped her cheek with the corner of her apron. I thought about what she had just said, then got up and walked down to the barn where Clay and Mr. Billings were helping Ginny with her 4-H lamb.

The Cochise County Fair was going to be held in September and Ginny was working hard to get her lamb ready. I walked up to where Mr. Billings and Clay were watching. She walked her lamb around in the pen, then set the lamb up for an imaginary judge. "Looks like she knows what she's doing," I said.

"That she does," Mr. Billings said. "Her momma was a good coach. When Norma was Ginny's age she did a lot of showing, first with lambs and then steers. The FFA and 4-H have been a part of this family for a long time."

"That's really something," I said. "I'll bet Mrs. Billings is very proud of Ginny."

"We all are," Mr. Billings said. "But I'm sure Norma is prouder than all of us. After all, she taught her everything she knew and Ginny has taken to it like a duck to water."

Clay said, "Maybe next year we should show a couple of steers."

Mr. Billings nodded. "That's not a bad idea, Clay."

"Where would we get the steers?" I asked.

Mr. Billings chuckled. "Heck Tyler you own some pretty nice cows now. Maybe one of them will have a good prospect for y'next March. It's for sure if you were able to sell one of 'em at the fair it would bring you more money than it would otherwise."

"I never thought of that." I looked at Clay. "Would you teach me how to get one ready to show?"

"Sure will," Clay said. "Besides, if we feed 'em both together at first they'll do better. Next year we can work up our rations in Ag-Class. We'll be having a section on feeds and feeding in the second quarter. We can put together a starting ration and then one to finish 'em off."

That was the first time I had seen Clay excited about something in awhile. I was hoping that our roping and now the possibility of showing steers next year would improve his state of mind.

Ginny finished working with her lamb and put him back in his pen and fed him a little. It seemed like the lamb knew that working well for Ginny would get him a little grain. As I watched Ginny care for her lamb, I realized she was intent on making sure everything was done well. I realized it would probably be a good idea to get involved in 4-H. It seemed to me the program really had a lot to offer.

Mr. Billings said, "Would you boys mind riding up to Big Horn Canyon and checking the cows up there? Maybe on the way back you wouldn't mind looking at the windmill in the Morgan pasture. It's going to start warming up soon and we want to make sure it's working well."

"Sure, Dad," Clay replied. "It's a great day for a ride."

Ginny must have heard the plan. She asked,

"Would you two mind if I tagged along?"

"Not at all," Clay said. "We'll head out right after lunch."

"Yeah, Mom has a roast on," I said. "And she really knows how to prepare one."

Mr. Billings chuckled. "I haven't seen much she didn't fix well!"

"She's a cook all right," I said. We all headed to the house.

After we ate Clay and I went down to the barn and saddled up. Ginny was right behind us, not about to be left behind.

It was about an hour ride over to Big Horn Canyon. We had plenty of time to talk as we rode along. I could tell that both of them needed a lot of encouragement regarding their Mother. I never knew I could have so much to say regarding what they were experiencing. I guess losing Dad had caused me to have feelings I didn't realize I had. I'm not sure where the thought came from but I said, "There are a lot of things in life that don't seem fair. We just have to make the most of what we have."

When I said that, silence overtook both of them. We must have ridden for twenty minutes before either of them said a thing.

When Clay finally spoke it wasn't about his mother or what I had said. He reined his horse to a stop, then pulled out his field glasses and scanned the canyon ahead of us. "Well, there are about a dozen head right up that draw. Let's check 'em out."

Ginny and I followed Clay as he rode out. He seemed to be in a completely different place in time. He was deep in thought, very quiet and matter of fact when he spoke.

We rode Big Horn Canyon all afternoon and found most of the cattle we were looking for. One thing we weren't ready to come across were fresh trails made by illegal border crossers. Along some of the trails were backpacks, clothing and plastic milk jugs littering the countryside.

Clay looked down at the mess as we rode along. He looked disgusted. "These people have no respect for this country. No telling what all they were carrying. We know for a fact they've used this area to smuggle drugs through."

"Doesn't the Border Patrol come out here?" I asked.

"Yeah… they do." Clay said. "But there's not enough of them it seems. A lot of the ranchers along the border have asked for the military to be deployed to stop this sort of thing."

"Yeah," I said. "One day Granddad took me for a ride out Geronimo Trail. He told me about the problem. He even took his rifle with him on the drive."

"That was a smart thing to do," Clay said. "Things could get pretty bad out here if the government doesn't do something about it. It seems they'd rather send our troops over to Iraq or Afghanistan."

Man did that ever hit home. "Yeah," I said. "If they'd have sent my dad out here to protect our own country he might still be alive."

As we rode back to the ranch that day we got into a pretty heavy discussion regarding what we had just witnessed. We were all in agreement that the government had to do something to get the situation under control. It was a disappointment to all of us that these things were allowed to continue. No wonder so many ranchers were in fear of keeping their operations intact. Not only were they faced with fluctuating cattle prices, drought, and livestock diseases, but they were now faced with illegal activities out of Mexico. To top it off, our government wasn't doing much to get it stopped.

Chapter Fifteen
Rodeos and Team Ropings

Despite the fact Clay was battling bouts of depression we were able to continue practicing as a team. We practiced continually and were becoming formidable. Nubbin and I were starting to understand each other better too. When I'd first started riding him it seemed like we just didn't jell. He would work one way and I'd be working in a completely different manner. I found out quickly that working with a new horse is a lot like working with people you've just met. It takes awhile to understand their ways.

Nubbin was well trained before I'd started riding him. It just took me awhile to get used to him. In time we became a good team and our understanding of each other's abilities only enhanced the abilities of our partners, Clay and Woodrow. When Clay rode into the headers box on Woodrow, that palomino stud was all business.

We practiced almost everyday, making at least seven or eight runs. Ernesto and Diego would keep the steers loaded in the chute, and Clay and I would rope. Now and then Clay and I would give our horses a break and load the chute for Ernesto and Diego. We all seemed to be getting plenty of good practice. Mr. Billings would sometimes come down to the roping pen to watch us. He'd let us know if he saw us doing something wrong. It was good having someone like him as our coach. He'd always say, "Practice like you're doing it for real." That was sound advice, and I began to apply it to a lot of things over time.

Before school let out for that year Clay and I had been to a couple of ropings and a high school rodeo. We'd been doing well in the team roping, but I had yet to win my first buckle. That May we made it to one of the bigger rodeos, but Clay and I had our minds set on the Arizona High School Championship, which was to be held in June.

Rodeoing like we were, I remember thinking how much I would have liked my dad to see me accomplish these new things. At times I even forgot he was actually gone and I would think, *Wait 'till Dad sees this.* Then I'd realize he was no longer with us and he wouldn't see my accomplishments. Never a day went by that I didn't think of him and wonder whether somehow he could see what I was doing.

Having the new rig Granddad had bought me made it a lot easier for us to get down the road to the ropings and rodeos. Clay and I would load up Nubbin and Woodrow and set sail. Every time we went, there was always a new adventure.

When Ginny went along with her barrel horse Lilly, it was a bonus. She had quite a few friends who were can chasers and it always gave Clay and me time to get to know them. Sometimes that led to some mighty interesting conversations. There were times though that Ginny seemed to get upset if I showed too much attention to anyone else in particular.

All seemed to be going well. Clay and I were beginning to click in the team roping. However, I could still see the turmoil he was going through concerning his mother's plight. At times he seemed to handle it fairly well, but then he would drop back into a state of depression.

For the life of me I couldn't figure out what I could do to help my friend. Then it came to me. One night on our journey from North Carolina to Arizona, I remember lying in bed thinking about my father and the strength he always showed. I had thought, *What am I going to do now without him?* And it had come to me like he was there in that dark motel room talking to me. He'd said, "Do things with strength, courage and determination, and soon your future will be manifested."

I remember sitting up in bed, looking around to see whether he was really there or whether it was just a figment of my imagination.

Perhaps I could convey those thoughts to Clay. Maybe—just maybe—it might help him. But how could I bring up such a sensitive subject?

I pondered on it for several days. Then one day as we were traveling to another roping I looked at Clay. "Clay, I know you're terribly worried about your mother. I can tell it weighs heavily on your mind most of the time and I worry for you. You're the best friend I've ever had and I love your family as though they were my very own, so I need to say something. I don't want you to think I'm being insensitive to what's going on with your mother. God knows I'd never say or do anything to hurt you."

Clay looked at me. "What are you trying to say, Tyler?"

"It's like this, Clay. I've been terribly concerned about you and how the situation is affecting you. "

Clay shot back at me. "I know you're worried about our winning at the ropings. Don't worry. I won't lose your entries."

"For heaven's sake, Clay, I'm not worried about that. I'm worried about you! I've been thinking about something that happened to me after we heard my dad was killed. We were on the way out here. I had no idea what was going to happen to me. One night I was lying in bed thinking about my dad and wondering just what was going to happen to me next. I was going into a situation completely foreign to anything I'd ever experienced before. As I lay there in the darkness,

144

I could hear the diesel drone of eighteen wheelers going down the highway. I was scared and missing my dad. Then I heard his voice as though he was in the room. He said I should do things with strength, courage and determination and soon my future would be manifested.

"Now Clay, I know you're going through a very tough time right now, but I also know you'll come out of it extremely well. Just remember my dad's words and carry them with you. I have and they've really made me realize there are better times ahead. There will be for you also. You just have to have faith in the Lord and in what you're trying to accomplish."

I could tell what I'd said had hit Clay pretty hard. He didn't say much for quite awhile. As we were about to enter Buckeye, he said, "Are you hungry? Maybe we should stop at the Waffle House and grab a bite."

He'd heard what I had said and was dwelling on it. Somehow I knew he'd pull through these periods of depression and his life would take on new meaning. He wouldn't totally lose thoughts of his mother's condition or the inevitable, but perhaps he would be able reflect on things in a way that he could bring new meaning to his own life and to the lives of his sister and father.

The roping went well for us that weekend. We covered our expenses. Clay and Woodrow performed well. Unfortunately I legged our last steer in a three-steer average and cost us second place. But it seemed Clay was thinking about things a little better. Maybe now he'd be able to put what he was facing in a better light.

We were progressing well as a team. Back at the ranch Ernesto and Diego were working to keep us in fresh Corrientes for the practices. They would keep a few in for a couple of days and then run them out to the big pasture and bring in a few more. Fresh cattle really made a difference in our practice.

One evening after practice Pete called us over to the barn for a conference. "Boys, you've been pretty consistent at your practicing and it's paid off at the ropings. I think it's time you start planning on what you want to do this summer."

Clay looked at me and then at his dad. "We've been talking about that, Dad. Tyler and I would like to hit a couple more jackpots, then enter up in the Arizona High School Championship in June."

I said, "Yeah, Mr. Billings, and if we qualify there we'd like to hit the High School National Finals in July."

"That sounds like some pretty good planning," Pete said. "Clay, are you going to enter the bulldoggin' too?"

"I'd like to," Clay replied. "I'll need to look for

146

another doggin' horse though. Diego said he knew of a good one in Tucson. Might be able to pick him up right."

"What do you know about the horse?" Pete asked.

"They call him Chivo. He's a pretty seasoned doggin' horse from what they say."

"Maybe you'd better try him out, and soon. June will be here before you know it. You don't want to show up with a horse you haven't been working with."

"I'll get Diego to see when we can go up and try him," Clay replied.

"Okay. Do you have anything else in mind other than the State Finals?"

Clay nodded. "We thought we might head up to the International Finals Youth Rodeo in Shawnee, Oklahoma. It's in July."

"We can take my rig," I said.

"That's a pretty good haul," Pete said. "But I guess y'gotta get your feet wet sometime. Do you think your mom will be all right with a trip like that?"

I nodded. "I think she'll be okay with it. After all, it won't have been our first road trip. I'll clear it with her this evening."

"Well, boys, you have your work cut out for you. You'd better get on it." Pete seemed proud that we had put thought into our plans for the summer. On the other hand it seemed he had concerns about us striking out on our own like that.

That evening I approached Mom with the plans. She too was very concerned about things, but went ahead with it. I guess by that time she had developed enough confidence in Clay and me that she knew we'd use good judgment on a long trip. She also knew we had discussed everything with Mr. Billings. That alone gave her a better feeling about the ordeal.

That week Clay and I went to work getting our plans together. One thing we had overlooked was that if we qualified for the National High School Finals at State, we'd have to get back to enter up right after the IFYR in Shawnee. We might have to have someone drive our horses from Shawnee to Farmington, New Mexico. Clay and I would have to fly to Durango, Colorado, and get down to Farmington to enter up. We decided to talk it over with Mr. Billings.

After talking it over with him he decided that perhaps we should ask Diego to go with us to Shawnee. He could bring the horses back to Farmington. Mr. Billings said he and Ernesto could handle things around the ranch. We talked it over with Diego, and it was set. He'd go to Shawnee with us and get the horses to Farmington for the

Nationals—if we qualified at State.

Now all we had to do was buy that doggin' horse Chivo and continue practicing. We were pushing the time envelope. The Arizona State Finals were closing in on us.

Chapter Sixteen
The Summer of 2002

Clay purchased Chivo from a retired dogger who had been to the National Finals Rodeo in 2000. Chivo was all business when he backed into the box. In no time they were working well together. Pete hazed for them. Clay began doggin' five or six steers every time we practiced.

We were also becoming very consistent during our roping practices. Our confidence was high and our times were getting better. Placing well at the upcoming Arizona State Finals seemed to be a viable expectation. After all, we'd already roped well against some of the teams we'd be facing.

It became evident to me that my life had taken on more changes than I'd ever believed possible after losing Dad. I had become a ranch cowboy and an FFA and 4-H member. I had a cow-calf operation going and I was becoming a pretty fair heeler and was going to the Arizona High School Finals.

Back then we didn't know what a bucket list was. However, I was putting one together without even realizing it. One thing I hadn't accomplished was winning a trophy buckle. That was high on my list of things to do. I hadn't forgotten the first time

I walked into the Billing's home and saw the trophy cases full of buckles. Since then I had gotten close to winning one a couple of times, but it had eluded me. With our well-laid plans for a summer of rodeo, I was determined to win at least one buckle.

The Arizona State Finals were getting close. Knowing that, I became even more concerned about Mrs. Billings. Clay and I knew she wanted desperately to watch us in action. The big question was whether she would she be strong enough to make the trip. She was trying hard to stay positive. However, the dreaded disease was stealing her strength. She was very frail. It was becoming difficult for her to move about, even with Mom or Ginny's assistance.

Ginny had pretty much given up on the idea of running barrels at the finals. She seemed to be intent on caring for her mother. She was selfless and pretty much had given up on anything extra for herself.

Pete seemed to pour himself into his ranch work. It was like he was shielding himself from the seriousness of Mrs. Billings' sickness by working harder. He also became more demanding of our work schedule. Clay and I were always up and at it shortly after sun-up. Pete knew how important our rodeo plans were, and he allowed us ample time in the practice pen. When I look back on it, I think the hard work and having to make our practice time count made us even more competitive.

We had sent in our entries the first of May. Clay had entered the bulldoggin', calf roping and team roping with me. I only entered the team roping. Our plans seemed to be coming together well.

The week before we left for Globe, Mom and Pete took Mrs. Billings to see her doctor in Tucson. It was a grueling trip for her, but the doctor wanted to exam her before she went on the trip. The doctor gave them specific orders to make sure she didn't overdo things. She was to get plenty of rest when she wasn't at the rodeo grounds.

Clay and I practiced right up to the day before we left for the finals. We took my rig with Woodrow, Nubbin and Chivo. Mr. Billings drove Mrs. Billings and Mom and Ginny up in his car. My grandparents also drove up. Granddad told us there was no way he was going to miss that rodeo.

As long as I live I'll never forget the feeling I had as we made that journey. It was my first trip to a rodeo of that significance. It seemed surrealistic to me.

We made it to the rodeo grounds and stabled our horses, then walked over to find out when we would be up. Clay was up in the doggin' in Friday's afternoon performance. We were up in the team roping that evening. Clay was up in the calf roping slack Saturday morning. The final performance and short goes would be on Sunday.

After checking out what barrel racers were there, we headed to the motel. Everyone was there and Mrs. Billings was resting. Everyone else was taking it easy and watching TV.

As we walked into Pete's room he looked at Clay. "Well, how does it look?"

"Not bad, Dad," Clay replied. "We're pretty well spaced out in the performances. Looks like there'll be about sixty teams, twenty bulldoggers and forty-six calf ropers. We've seen most 'em before."

"Sounds good," Mr. Billings said. He looked at me. "How you feelin' about it, Tyler?"

"I believe I'm set. I mean from the looks of things all we have to do is rope like we've been practicing. I have to admit though, I do have some butterflies. I just hope they don't turn into eagles tomorrow."

Mr. Billings chuckled. "You'll be okay. Everyone gets a little nervous before a rodeo. Just remember to concentrate on what you're doin'. Don't let anyone distract you and you'll be fine. By the way, did you know they're awarding buckles for the fast goes each day and trophy saddles to the average winners?"

"Why no!" I said. "Thanks, Mr. Billings. I need all the encouragement I can get. I'd sure like to pick up one of those buckles!"

That evening we all went to a nice Mexican Food Restaurant—all except Mrs. Billings and Mom. They stayed back at the motel. Granddad ordered some tacos to take back to them.

Mr. Billings, Clay and I headed for the rodeo grounds early the next morning. After feeding and watering the horses we walked over to see whether there had been any changes in the event schedule —there hadn't been—and then we found a concession stand for a bite to eat. Afterward, we went back and saddled Woodrow and Nubbin. Clay put a halter on Chivo to pony him around a little. We wanted to get them out of their stalls for awhile to make sure they didn't tie up. After a few laps around the arena we hit the wash rack. The horses seemed to have made the trip without any problems.

The afternoon performance was on us before we realized it. Clay and I watched the bareback rides, then went over and saddled Chivo. Clay had lined up Walt Grayson, one of the other bulldoggers, to haze for him.

Shortly we heard the announcer say, "Okay, you doggers... be gettin' ready."

Clay rode over behind the chute and sat there on Chivo, watching the other doggers going out ahead of him. He seemed to be in a zone, as though he'd blocked out everything around him. I had never seen him so focused.

The announcer called out, "Your next bulldogger in this performance will be Clay Billings. This cowboy has been around since he was knee high to a jackrabbit. He comes from a long line of rodeo champions. He's one to watch."

Clay rode into the box and backed Chivo into the corner. Walt Grayson was in the hazer's box. I'll never forget how intense Clay was. Chivo was focused on the chute, ears pointed forward, and he looked wound tight as the main spring on a Swiss watch. You could tell this wasn't his first rodeo. Clay nodded and Chivo sprang forward just as the barrier shot open. Walt moved the horned steer in just right. Clay was on the Corriente with precise movement. He set the steer perfectly and moved with the precision of a champion wrestler. The steer was on his side in a flash.

Clay got up and dusted himself off as he began walking back toward the chute.

The announcer excitedly said, "Folks, you've just witnessed a run that any pro going down the road would be proud of. Clay threw that steer in four point two seconds flat. Great run, cowboy!"

Modestly, Clay raised his right arm over his

head and walked out of the arena, knowing that if anyone was going to beat that time he'd have to hustle.

I learned a lot about my good friend that day. When he went into an arena to compete, there was no fooling around. He performed the best he could, and when he did well he showed a lot of class. There was no over-exuberant show of celebration—just a young man showing the humility of someone who one day might make it to the finals in Vegas.

If only I could follow his example.

Walt led Chivo over and handed the reins to Clay. "That was a great run, Clay!"

"Thanks, Walt. I couldn't've done it without your help. You hazed that steer perfectly. I owe you a milkshake."

"I look forward to it," Walt said as he rode away.

Mr. Billings was waiting for us at the stalls. He had a big smile on his face as we walked up. "That was one fine run, Clay." He patted Clay on the shoulder.

"Thanks, Dad. Did Mom see it? I was determined to make her proud."

"She sure did, Son. It brought tears to her eyes."

"We'll even do better in the team roping," Clay said. "I've made up my mind this rodeo is for our Moms. They put up with a lot from us at times. We'd better do something right for them." He began to unsaddle Chivo.

"You boys better take it easy for awhile," Mr. Billings said. "When that evening performance gets here you need to be rested and ready to rope. That team roping looks like it could get wolfy."

"That's for sure," Clay replied. "But we'd like to watch this go-around in the team roping."

We walked over and sat behind the roping chutes for the team roping. After watching every team that roped we felt pretty confident that if we roped like we'd been practicing, we'd probably place pretty well. There were only five clean runs and the fastest time was a ten-two.

They played The National Anthem at six o'clock right on schedule. Clay and I had brought a practice dummy along, so we took some warm-up practice for a while before getting Woodrow and Nubbin saddled.

Before I knew it the announcer was calling teams for the performance. Clay and I selected our ropes out of the rope bags and worked with them a little.

He looked over at me. "We can do this, Tyler. Just focus on the steer and be ready when I turn him off. Rope like you did when we were in the practice pen."

I tried to work up a confident smile. "Okay,

Clay. I'll be there."

When I heard the announcer call our names my stomach knotted up. I took a deep breath and let it out to calm my nerves. Here I was in the biggest rodeo of my team roping experience.

I rode Nubbin into the heeler box and backed him into the corner. He was ready. He looked straight at the steer standing in the chute. Clay was set and he looked over at me as if to say *Are you ready?*

I nodded.

He looked at the chute hand. "Let 'em go."

The gate sprang open. Woodrow had Clay in position in three strides. Clay roped the Corriente clean and set him perfectly with a good even movement to the left. By the time I had made two swings with my loop Nubbin had me in position. On the third swing I let it go and set the best heel loop I'd ever thrown. I dallied and we faced off. Clay looked across at me with a big smile. Even though I was still in a slight daze, I could tell by his smile we must have had a good time.

The announcer said, "That's a six-two, folks! Give those cowboys a hand. They're the new fast time for the day. That was some fine roping."

After Clay retrieved his rope at the stripping chute, he rode out of the arena to where I was sitting on Nubbin waiting for him. He still had that big smile on his face.

He said, "All *right*, partner! You really put that one together!"

"Thanks," I said. "I thought I was going to explode until I saw you nod for the steer. Then everything started to come together. I guess we did pretty well. What do you think?'

"No doubt about it, Tyler... no doubt about it."

After we unsaddled and put Woodrow and Nubbin in their stalls, we walked over to where the family was seated. Mrs. Billings smiled at us and told us how proud of us she was. She gave us both a big hug and a kiss on the cheek. I knew we had pleased both of our mothers very much.

Granddad and Grandmother said they couldn't believe how far I'd come since working with Pete and Clay. I told them I had two of the best coaches in Arizona. I knew if it hadn't been for them there was no telling what I'd be doing.

Pete chimed in. "I don't know whether you boys realize it yet, but you've both picked up buckles today."

With the excitement I was feeling about our run, I had totally forgotten that they were awarding buckles for the fast times. I silently let it sink in. *My gosh! I finally won my first buckle!* I could hardly believe it. Was I dreaming or what?

That night after the performance was over

Mom and Ginny drove Mrs. Billings back to the motel. It had been a long day for her and she was extremely tired. The rest of us found a café and ate supper.

While we were eating, the day's results were the main conversation. Pete emphasized how important it was for us to maintain our momentum. "Don't get over confident. Remember, it isn't over until the last run's been made."

After supper Clay and I decided to go to the rodeo dance. From what we'd seen that day there were plenty of can chasers to dance with. We went back to the motel to shower and change clothes. It would improve our chances with the gals if we got some of the arena dust off.

While we were there we asked Ginny whether she wanted to tag along. It took some convincing, but she finally relented and went with us. She really needed a break. She'd been helping her mother continuously for quite sometime. It was obvious it was taking a toll on her.

We were at the rodeo grounds early the next morning. Clay was up in the calf roping slack that morning. After Woodrow had eaten, Clay saddled him and rode him around in the arena to warm him up. Around seven-thirty the announcer was calling for the calf ropers. Clay rode over a waited behind the chute. I walked over and sat behind the chute to watch his run.

There were fifteen ropers ahead of him. I knew better than to try and talk to Clay. He was all business. Clay watched as each roper made his run. Only eight roped their calves and the fastest time was ten-two.

Finally the announcer called for Clay Billings. I could sense Clay's intense determination as he backed Woodrow into the box. They were both poised, concentrating on the calf in the chute.

The chute hand had to straighten the calf around so he was standing on all fours and facing forward. Clay waited intensely and as soon as the calf was set he nodded.

Clay was moving forward as the calf sprang out of the chute. They moved toward the calf at a run. Clay made two swings with his loop and let it fly. As the loop spun the calf around, Woodrow was setting up working the calf perfectly as Clay flanked and tied him. It was teamwork in its purist form. In a split second Clay had made the tie and he was reaching for the sky. The flagger dropped the flag. Clay walked back and mounted Woodrow. He nudged the palomino forward, giving the calf some slack. The flagger rode up and gave the calf six seconds to struggle loose. No way —the calf had been tied hard and fast. It was a clean run.

The announcer came over the PA system. "Well folks, this cowboy came ready to rope. He just tied that calf in seven-four. That's the fast time so far in this morning's slack."

Clay and I watched as six more ropers made their runs. They were all pushing hard to beat Clay's seven-four. Two pushed too hard and made sloppy ties and their calves kicked loose in the six seconds. The flagger waved them off and the announcer announced, "No time" over the PA. One tied his calf in nine-six, and the others missed and got a no time.

Clay had the fast time in the slack that morning. Now came the wait for the afternoon and evening performances. It was a long wait that day but by the end of the evening performance Clay had the fast time in the calf roping. He had fast time in the bulldoggin' and we had fast time in the team roping going into the short go on Sunday. That wasn't bad for a couple of boys from Douglas.

By the end of the short goes and finals on Sunday, Clay had won the bulldoggin' and placed second in the calf roping. By the grace of God and a two-second margin, Clay and I had won the team roping. What a weekend that was! We managed to take home some good paychecks, three buckles and two saddles. Clay had qualified in the calf roping and bulldoggin' for the National

High School Finals and I was in the team roping with him. It was set. We'd go to Shawnee, then back to the Nationals. What more could we ask for?

Personally I felt as though I had won the lottery. I couldn't believe I had actually won that elusive trophy buckle and, to top it off, a saddle. It was all beyond my imagination. Who would have believed an army brat from Fort Bragg would have done something like that? I wished Dad had been there to see it.

When we returned to the ranch, Ernesto and Diego were anxious to hear all about the weekend. They were extremely happy when we showed them our winnings. It seemed to me they even began to show me a little more attention. It was like they wanted to help me even more with my roping. I guess they knew Clay was going to do well and they wanted me to be right there with him. Whatever it was, I really appreciated their extra advice and help

Our work and rodeo practice continued and we attended a summer 4-H meeting. It was getting close to the time we'd be leaving for Shawnee. We were confident and ready to go.

Granddad and Grandmother came out to the ranch the weekend before we left. Pete smoked a couple of briskets. Mom, Ginny and Grandmother fixed all the trimmings. Ginny baked a couple of her famous pies. It was a momentous get together. Everyone was there. Ernesto and Diego even brought their families out.

The table was set under some large oak trees in the back yard that gave us plenty of shade. There was a light breeze blowing out of the Southwest. It was apparent that we might be getting some rain in the near future. It was a perfect day for a picnic.

Clay paid special attention to his Mom that day. She was trying hard to enjoy everyone's company, but you could see in her eye she was very tired. She tried to eat, but couldn't. I could tell Clay was extremely worried about her.

With weakness in her voice Mrs. Billings said, "Katherine... would you and Ginny help me into the house?" Mom and Ginny moved quickly to assist Mrs. Billings.

"Are you okay?" Clay asked.

Trembling as they helped her to her feet, she replied, "Yes Clay... I'm fine."

Mom and Ginny helped her, steadying her as they as they slowly walked toward the house.

For the next couple of days I could tell Clay really didn't have his mind on practicing. He was thinking about his Mom. The day before we were to leave for Shawnee he came to me. "Tyler, do you think it's okay for me to leave right now? I mean... well, Mom hasn't been doing all that well this past week."

I could tell by looking at him he was terribly worried. I said, "Listen, Brother, if you feel we ought to skip this one it's fine by me. I want you to do what you think is best."

"Well, I'm just concerned about Mom. I'd hate to be away if she needed me."

"Tell you what. Why don't you and your dad have a little meeting with her? Just the three of you. Explain your concerns and let them help you make a decision."

"That's a good idea, Tyler. I'll do that."

That evening Clay asked his dad to join him in his mother's room. They were in there for quite awhile discussing things. Clay came out of her room alone. It was obvious he'd been crying.

"Are you okay?" I asked.

"I... I think so, Tyler."

"What did you decide?"

"Well, Mom sort'a insisted that I go on to Shawnee. She said she'd come out of this bad spell pretty soon. She convinced me to go on and go."

"Listen, Clay, I'll be there for you, and I'm with you whatever you finally decide."

"I'll let you know for sure in the morning," Clay said. "I'm a little bushed right now. Think I'll hit the rack. See'ya in the morning."

With that he slowly walked toward his bedroom.

The next morning during our morning chores we weren't saying much. Clay seemed to be somewhere else. He managed the chores like he was on automatic pilot. Finally he said, "Tyler, if Mom and Dad think I should go on to Shawnee, I think that's what I'll do. Besides, we already entered up. It would be a shame for us to draw out."

"Okay, partner... if that's what you want to do, I'm with you."

Two days later we were packed and ready to go. Diego was set and everything was in order. We all met in the house in Mrs. Billings' room for a farewell. She looked up. "Pete, would you send these boys on with a prayer for their safe journey?"

Surprised at her request, Mr. Billings said, "Sure, Honey." He bowed his head and we followed his lead. He said, "Lord, we are thankful for all that you bring into our lives. We know that all we have is through your graciousness." He paused, then continued with a trembling voice. "Lord, please bless my sweet wife Norma. Give her strength and comfort her during her illness. We ask that you'll be with our boys as they make this trip to Shawnee. Please give them and their horses a safe journey. Thankin' you again, Lord, for all we have from your hands. Amen."

Mrs. Billings looked up at her husband., tears running down her gaunt face. Trembling, she said,

"Thank you, Pete. That was a good one." She looked over at us. "Now you boys be careful and keep your minds on business. I'd like to see some more nice sterling silver trophy buckles come back with you."

"We will, Mom," Clay said as he leaned down and kissed her on the cheek.

I reached down and held her hand. "Mrs. Billings, we'll bring you back some buckles."

"Give me a kiss, cowboy."

I looked at Clay. He had a grin on his face. "You better give her a kiss, or she'll never forgive you."

I leaned down and gave Mrs. Billings a kiss on the cheek. "Thanks, Mrs. Billings. That really meant a lot to me."

"You're mine too," she said.

We all said our goodbyes and the three of us drove away from the ranch. Shawnee, Oklahoma, was our destination.

Chapter Seventeen
The Unexpected

We hit highway eighty and turned east toward Road Forks. Twenty-five minutes later we passed the Geronimo Surrender Monument at Apache. I looked south toward Skeleton Canyon. Large dark clouds were beginning to build. "Looks like the ranch might get some rain today." I don't think Clay even heard what I said. He just stared straight ahead at the openness ahead of us. Mentally he was at the ranch with his mother. I could only hope he'd pull it together in Shawnee.

We stopped in Deming to get some diesel and grab a quick bite to eat, then took State Route 26 to Hatch, New Mexico, home of the infamous Hatch Chili Festival. We hit Interstate 25 right out of Hatch and headed north.

As we were nearing Albuquerque, my cell phone rang.

"Hello," I said. "Yeah, Mom. Everything's going well. No problems, why?"

I listened to Mom intently. "I can't believe this!"

Clay looked startled. "What's going on, Tyler?" The look on my face must have been telling. He looked at me with a terrified expression. "Is it Mom?"

"Give me a minute, Clay. Let me hear what Mom's saying."

I listened, then spoke into the phone. "Okay Mom, I will." I quickly ended the call.

Terrified, Clay yelled, "What's going on, Tyler?"

"They've taken your mom to Tucson. She slipped into a coma about an hour after we left the ranch."

Clay began to well up. With a trembling voice, he asked," Is she okay? She hasn't died, has she, Tyler?"

"No, she's in a coma. They've taken her to University Medical Center in Tucson. Mom wants me to put you on a flight back to Tucson when we get into Albuquerque."

Diego took the exit that directed traffic to the airport. As we drove up to the terminal I said, "Diego you won't get this trailer in that parking garage. Just drive around until you see me come back out. Clay, don't worry about your duffel bag. Let's just get you on the first flight to Tucson."

There was a short line at the ticket counter. As we got to the ticket agent, I said, "Ma'am, we have an emergency here and need a one-way ticket to Tucson on your first available flight."

After I briefly explained the situation to her, she said. "We have a Tucson flight leaving in twenty minutes. Does he have any baggage?"

"No Ma'am," I said.

I handed her Clay's drivers license and she printed the ticket and the boarding pass. "That will be one-hundred fifty dollars. He'll have to hurry to the gate as they'll be boarding soon."

I handed her my credit card and it was done.

Clay was still in a daze. I couldn't imagine what he was thinking. I said, "Look Clay, you've got to hold it together. I'll make sure you get on the plane and then call Mom with the flight information and your arrival time in Tucson. She'll pick you up."

Clay looked at me with little expression. Speaking slowly he said, "Thank you, Tyler." He checked through security and walked down the corridor to the gate where he boarded his flight.

I couldn't seem to bring myself to leave the terminal until I saw the plane taxi out.

Diego was pulling up when I walked out. I jumped in the pick-up as he stopped. "Well, we'd better head back to the ranch."

"Is Mrs. Billings going to be okay?" Diego asked.

"It's hard to say, Diego. They just don't know. Mom just said she was in a coma and they had flown her to Tucson Medical Center."

"My gosh," Diego said. "I hope Mr. Billings and Ginny are okay."

Diego headed the rig back to the interstate and

we headed south and then west, not knowing what the situation would be when we got to the ranch.

When we stopped in Lordsburg to top off with fuel, I called Mom. "Hello, Mom. Did Clay get there? That's good. How's he doing? Well, he was very upset when he got on the plane as well. We're in Lordsburg. We should be to the ranch in an hour or so. Please keep us informed on everything. Okay Mom, we will. I'll call you when we get to the ranch."

The ride to the ranch seemed to take forever. It was dusk when we pulled in. Ernesto came walking out of the barn. He'd been doing the evening chores. Diego pulled up to where he was standing.

"Howdy, Ernesto," I said.

He walked up to us and shook our hands. "This has been one heck of a day."

"What happened?" I asked.

"Well, after you left, Ginny ran up to the barn yelling for Mr. Billings. She said her mom was talking to her and Mrs. Roland and just seemed to fall into a deep sleep. She said Mrs. Roland tried to wake her but she didn't wake up. Mr. Billings ran to the house to check on her. Then he carried her out to the car and they drove her to Douglas." He shrugged. "That's about it."

"I'd better try to get Mom on the phone," I said.

I walked toward the house and they began to unload the horses.

That was one phone call I'll never forget. Mom said Mrs. Billings probably had a stroke prior to falling into the coma, and she wasn't responding to treatment.

When we finished talking I went back and told Ernesto and Diego what I'd been told. "I'm heading to Tucson."

I arrived at Tucson Medical Center about nine that night. Everyone was in a waiting room near the intensive care unit. When I walked in Mom stood up and walked over to me and hugged me.

"I'm so glad you got here," she said.

I walked over to Mr. Billings and Clay, shook their hands and patted them on the shoulder, "Are you doing all right?"

Mr. Billings looked up at me. "I really don't know how to answer you, Tyler. I feel like my insides are being ripped out. It all happened so fast. One minute she was talking to your mom and Ginny, and the next minute she was in this coma."

"What has the doctor said?" I asked.

"Not very much," Mr. Billings replied. "He just said they had to do some tests... a CAT scan and others to see what caused the abrupt onset of the coma."

"How long has it been since you spoke with the doctor?" I asked.

"A couple of hours."

The doctor walked in as Mr. Billings and I were talking. He walked over to Mr. Billings. "Mr. Billings, we have the results of the CAT scan and some blood tests. I have consulted with Doctor Lansing, one of our neurosurgeons here at TMC. We believe we know what caused the sudden onset of the stroke."

"What happened?" Mr. Billings asked.

"Would you like to go to a more private area?" the doctor asked.

Pete looked around the room. "Sir, the people here are all family either by blood relation or love for Norma. They're all heartsick and want to know what has happened." He paused. "So no... everyone here needs to hear what you have to say."

The doctor looked at all of us. "It appears that your wife had an inner-cranial bleed The cancer migrated to her brain, causing the blood to thicken. That caused the brain to bleed, which in turn brought about the stroke and coma."

Mr. Billings was unable to speak.

Mom asked the doctor, "Will she be able to recover from this?"

"She is in extremely critical condition. As I said, the cancer has metastasized. Her vitals are very weak. At this time we just can't predict what might happen."

Mr. Billings asked, "When will you know?"

"We will have a much better idea how she's responding to treatment over the next twelve hours. Right now there isn't anything that any of you can do. Perhaps you should go to a motel and try and get some rest."

"I'm not going anywhere!" Mr. Billings said gruffly. He looked at Mom. "Katherine, would you take the kids to a motel? I'll call you when I know more."

"Sure, Pete. Come on, kids, let's find a place to get some rest."

During all of that Clay never said a word. He just listened as though learning all he could about his mother's condition was the only important thing in the world.

We found a place to stay and turned in. Mom and Ginny were in one room and Clay and I shared the one next to them. It was a long night. I don't think anyone slept much. All I could think about was Mrs. Billings and about Mr. Billings staying right there with her. What love and devotion!

We were up early the next morning. Mom took us to a nice restaurant for breakfast, and then we headed to TMC. When we arrived in the waiting room Mr. Billings wasn't there. Mom went to the desk and asked whether they could tell her where Pete was.

The nurse said, "Please return to the waiting room and I'll page the doctor."

I'm not sure exactly what made me feel the way I did when the doctor walked in. He walked over to Mom. "Mrs. Roland, Pete asked me to speak with you this morning. My name is Doctor Givens."

Mom's face went pale. With a trembling voice she asked, "How is Norma? Where's Pete?"

" Pete is with his wife. He wanted to be with her for awhile before seeing all of you."

By that time we had all gathered around to find out what was being said.

Ginny was standing quietly next to Mom. Doctor Givens looked at her. "You must be Ginny. Your dad told me a lot about you last night. He's very proud of you and Clay." He looked at Clay and me. "And which one of you is Clay?"

"I am, Sir," Clay answered.

The doctor looked at me. "Then you must be Tyler." He looked at all of us. "During the night and early morning, Pete couldn't express enough just how proud he was of each of you. He really loves you kids." Doctor Givens seemed uneasy. "What I have to tell you is not a pleasant thing for me to do."

Clay said, "What happened, Doctor? Is Mom

okay?"

The doctor looked away for a moment, then took a deep breath. "Early this morning, Norma passed away. Pete was there with her throughout the night and he is with her now."

We all were in a daze, unable to bring ourselves to believe what we had just heard.

Ginny looked at Mom. "This can't be true! Mom couldn't have died!" Tears welled up and ran down her cheeks as she tried to catch her breath.

Mom put her arms around Ginny, trying to console her, but she was struggling with her own emotions. She helped Ginny sit down and continued to hug her.

I looked over at Clay. Silence had overtaken him. He turned, walked over and sat down, then leaned forward and cupped his face in his hands. As he looked up I could see the tears pooling in his eyes.

What can I do? I thought. I walked over to where he was sitting and sat next to him. "Clay?" I said quietly. "Is there something you want me to do?"

He just shook his head. Muffled sobs were coming from his hands, which were shielding his face.

Doctor Givens observed all of us, then said, "I'm going to inform Pete that I have spoken with all of you. He asked me to have you meet him in the chapel."

For a few minutes we just tried to adjust to the terrible news, then made our way to the hospital chapel. As Mr. Billings walked in, Ginny ran to meet him. Throwing her arms around him, she cried, "Oh Daddy! What are we going to do? Momma couldn't have died!" Ginny paused. "Can... can we at least see her?"

Mr. Billings drew her near. "I'm sure we can in just a little while." He paused. "For the first time in my life, I really don't know what to do. I've always had your mother there to help me make decisions during troubled times. I know she would want us to be strong now and be the kind of people she cherished."

Clay walked over to Pete and Ginny. His dad put an arm around him and the three of them held each other, not saying a word.

After several minutes Pete looked over at Mom. "I have some things I need to discuss with all of you."

"Sure, Pete."

We walked to a private room close to the chapel. As we entered, Mr. Billings said, "This whole situation is one I knew we would have to eventually face, but... but—"The raw emotions he was experiencing overcame him. We watched as he turned and faced the wall. His chest heaved as he tried to hold back emotions that had built up deep within him. He had tried to be strong for Clay and Ginny, but he wasn't able to control what he was feeling. Trying to hide his tears, he carefully wiped his eyes.

Mom walked over and put her hand on his shoulder. "It's all right, Pete. You don't have to hold everything in. We all understand."

With sadness in his voice, Pete quietly said, "Thank you, Katherine." He turned and walked over to where the rest of us were sitting. Mom followed him and they sat down.

"What I was going to say was, I'm going to need a lot of help. Katherine, I don't think I can bring myself to making the funeral arrangements alone. Would you mind helping me with them?"

"Of course, Pete."

"Thank you," Mr. Billings said.

That afternoon Mom made arrangements to have Mrs. Billings transported to a funeral home in Douglas. She and Ginny drove back to the ranch together. Mr. Billings and Clay rode back with me. It was a quiet, somber ride.

That was a week I'll never forget. Many memories of what we went through when we lost Dad flooded my mind. Again my granddad and grandmother were there to help. Granddad went with Mr. Billings to the funeral home to make all of the arrangements. Mom and Grandmother selected a nice dress for Mrs. Billings.

Ladies from neighboring ranches brought food to the ranch. Their husbands came to visit with Pete. Many of their youngsters whom we knew from FFA and 4-H also came with them. Watching them, I learned a great deal about country people. They did all they could to help the Billings family through that difficult time in their lives, yet they didn't intrude in any way.

The service was held at the funeral home chapel. Reverend Hertzman performed the ceremony, then asked others to relate stories about Mrs. Billings. It was obvious to everyone there that she was well loved and respected. The stories were both heartwarming and, at times, almost comical.

After the service Mrs. Billings was taken to Calvary Cemetery where she was laid to rest next to her mother and father.

The Cowbelles arranged the reception. They prepared a feast fit for a queen. I remember thinking that Mrs. Billings was probably regarded as a queen by many of them. Right up until she fell victim to that dreaded disease she was always there to help whoever needed a helping hand. That's just the kind of person Norma Billings was, always willing to help someone in need.

For the rest of the summer Clay and I stayed

pretty close to the ranch. We wanted to be there for Pete. He was having an extremely difficult time accepting the loss of his beloved wife. He lost a great deal of weight and his enthusiasm about the ranch seemed to wane.

Clay handled things a little different. He didn't say much about his mother, but you could always tell when he was thinking about her. It seemed like he was somewhere else. I knew better than to butt in when he drifted off like that. He would be in that state of mind for a while, then act like nothing had happened when he came out of it.

Mom continued to come out to the ranch and help Ginny with the housekeeping and would sometimes cook a nice meal for all of us. Ginny was always sad when Mom went back to town.

Sometimes Ginny would go back to town with her. Mom helped her with various projects like sewing or trying a new recipe. They even drove over to Sierra Vista and shopped at the mall and took in a movie. They became very close. It was like therapy for both of them. They had cared for Mrs. Billings night and day for many weeks, and now she was gone. They no doubt felt lost to a certain degree.

Clay and I continued our team roping practice, but we decided not to go to the High School National Finals. We had enjoyed making Mom and Mrs. Billings proud of us, but now that Mrs.

Billings was gone we had lost a certain amount of our enthusiasm. Besides, Mr. Billings needed help, and even though he had Ernesto and Diego there, Clay and I felt we should be around to do our share of the work.

Our senior year was drawing near, and it was time for the three of us to make sure our pre-registration was in order. We went to the school and checked our schedules. Clay and mine were okay and Ginny's was just like she had planned it.

We dropped by the Ag room to visit Miss Griggs. She was busy getting everything ready for the upcoming year. She was very enthusiastic and thought we had a good bunch of students coming up from eighth grade. While we were there she also expressed her sympathies to Clay and Ginny. She also complimented Clay and me on our win at the Arizona State Finals Rodeo. With performances like that she thought we'd be in line for rodeo scholarships at the end of our senior year.

Clay and I were hopeful for that as well. I knew in time we would be going to a lot more high school rodeos. Both of us knew that getting scholarships would help ease the financial burdens of college.

Chapter Eighteen
My Senior Year

Before we knew it we were back at old Douglas High. Clay and I were starting our senior year and Ginny was a junior. Even after the unsettling events of the past year we managed to regain our enthusiasm for school.

I knew Clay and Ginny would experience periods of loss and depression, just as I had when I lost my dad. It would only be natural. However, they were cut from strong fiber and managed to work their way through those difficult times.

Mom and I stayed in town the week prior to school starting. She wanted to make sure I had plenty of good clothes to wear. The ones I had been wearing all summer were getting threadbare. Last year when I shopped for school clothes it was Dockers and loafers. This year it was Wranglers and boots.

That first day back I waited for Clay and Ginny's bus to arrive. It was good to see them when they got off the bus. Some of Ginny's friends met up with her and they walked off together. Clay and I caught up on things that had gone on since we'd last seen each other.

I asked him how Mr. Billings was doing. He

said his dad had been working with Ginny and her 4-H lamb. Seems Ginny had really been putting in a lot of effort to get it ready for the fair in September. Clay said it was one of the best show lambs he'd seen in quite some time and he thought Ginny would do very well in showmanship and that her lamb was almost sure to take a blue ribbon and maybe even best of show.

About that time the first bell rang. Clay headed to math and I was off to my biology class. The only classes we had together that quarter were Spanish and our Ag classes in livestock production and shop.

My class schedule was such that I had extra time I could spend at the Ag shop. I wanted to rebuild some livestock handling equipment that had been discarded at the ranch. Mr. Billings told me that if I could put it back in working order I could sell it and use the money for my college fund. I was all for that. The calves I would sell would be a large part of what was needed, but I could always use more. I would also get credit for my Ag shop work.

That first week back was pretty exciting in Ag. Miss Griggs had a Power Point presentation that outlined subject matter we would be working on throughout the year and also major events we would be going to on judging teams and as a

184

chapter. I was happy to see that a great deal of the subject matter included livestock production, with emphasis on livestock diseases and feeds and feeding.

Clay and I were planning to show some steers at the county fair next year, so those subjects would help us accomplish that goal. We'd just have to wait and see what our calves looked like out of our next calf crop. We hoped we'd get a couple that had potential.

When fair time came around that September, Ginny was really serious about bringing home a blue ribbon for her lamb as well as one for showmanship. She had been on the right path for both. Her 4-H leader had given her a lot of good pointers on showmanship. However, Ginny knew a lot of it already. After all, her mother had been coaching her for a long time and Mrs. Billings really knew the ins and outs of showing livestock.

Ginny had worked hard with that Suffolk lamb. It was well groomed and she had walked it a lot. She practiced setting the lamb at least three to four times a week and pretended a judge was looking at it.

All of her hard work paid off that year at the fair. Her lamb received Best of Show and she won the Showmanship hands down. We were all very proud of her, especially Pete. It was an affirmation of the work his Norma had done with Ginny before she became ill.

Just before the fair, Miss Griggs told us we would have to start working on our chapter booth entry. The theme that year was New Technology in Agriculture. Agriculture had advanced a great deal by 2002. The possibilities were numerous for the competition.

Our chapter decided to display a computer as the center point of our entry. The title on the monitor was Advancement Through Research. We then had pointer strings coming from the monitor to photographs with text describing various advancements that had been made through the use of computers for research. There were photographs in the background depicting FFA students using computers in the classroom. Above the photographs was our slogan, *Our Future Begins Now*. Everyone who worked on the booth felt it was well done. The judges must have thought the same thing. Our chapter received the blue ribbon that year.

Even though Clay and I didn't have steers to show, we regarded the fair a success. In addition to our FFA chapter taking the blue ribbon for our booth entry, Ginny had won the showmanship and her lamb had done exceptionally well taking Grand Champion Lamb.

That year the three of us became very active in

FFA and 4-H. We were able to develop our knowledge of livestock production and management working in both organizations. We brought what we learned back to the ranch to help us with our livestock projects. The shop skills I learned helped me with my repairs on the discarded ranch equipment that Mr. Billings had given me.

Ginny continued with her household related projects as well. I think she felt it was her responsibility since her mother had passed away. She took particular interest in making sure the house was always well kept and she prepared good meals for her dad and Clay. Looking back on it I'm sure her activities in 4-H really enhanced her domestic development.

Clay and I were working pretty steady at the ranch on the weekends and practiced our roping as much as possible. Pete started pushing us to hit some ropings. He said we'd get complacent unless got back to competing. "It's one thing to continually practice in your own arena, but it's important to rope against other ropers. You keep a competitive edge that way."

We decided to go to an amateur roping the second weekend of October. It was a saddle roping in Tucson. We left early Saturday morning and were at the arena by seven-thirty. The roping was to start at eight. We made sure Woodrow and

Nubbin were okay, then went over and entered.

It was a three-steer average. You could enter three times, picking your partner. Clay and I entered three times as a team. We figured we'd have a good chance of winning a saddle that way.

By the time the entries closed there were a hundred and thirty teams entered. At fifty dollars a team entry fee, the pot looked pretty good, even though they took out thirty-percent for the cattle. You'd split around twenty-six hundred to win it, plus a saddle. That would give us more *dinero* for our college fund as well as entries for another roping.

We were charged and ready to rope.

Things went well. By the short go there were only thirty-nine teams left. Clay and I had the fastest time on two. When the announcer finally called us all we had to do was rope one in ten seconds. I could leg one and do that I thought. As luck would have it we drew a runner and I ended up leggin' the steer. We ended up third. We made back our entries and some fuel and food money and chalked it up to a good time. Pete was right about needing to be competing against other ropers. We might have won it had we been more focused.

Our 4-H leader told us about the 4-H Horse Show Finals coming up at the end of October. We decided to go. Ginny finally gave in and decided to enter the barrel racing. She hadn't practiced much that summer, but she kept her horse legged up. She practiced every chance she got up until time to leave for the Arizona State Fair and the 4-H Horse Show Finals.

Now that was really one heck of an experience. Not only were the events a hoot, but the fair itself was unbelievable. I'd never seen so many people in one place in my entire life.

Most of the 4-H finals had to do with showing horses. Ginny entered the barrel racing and Clay and I entered the team roping. He also entered the calf roping.

We had a great time. We did well in the events. Ginny placed second in the barrels, and Clay won the calf roping. He and I also won the team roping. It seemed like things were going our way for a change. I could definitely see a change in Clay. He seemed to be coming out of his bouts of depression.

We returned to Douglas and began our normal routines, going to our classes each day and attending FFA and 4-H meetings. The FFA meetings were normally held after school. Clay and Ginny would stay in town with Mom and me. I'd drive us to school the next day. They'd catch the bus back to the ranch after school.

Sometimes I'd ride out on the bus with them and we'd have a study session at the ranch. When we didn't have real pressing school business, Mr. Billings would sit and talk with us. The conversations normally focused on what was going on at the ranch.

Occasionally he would tell us stories about himself when he was a youngster on the ranch. I enjoyed those evenings in particular. I got good insight of why Mr. Billings was so dedicated to what he was doing in life. He was a cattleman through and through. Listening to his stories made me want to develop the same ethics that he had throughout his lifetime. You might say Mr. Billings was my mentor. He was a man who led by example.

That year citizenship was stressed in both the FFA and 4-H. I wondered whether perhaps Mr. Billings had developed some of his ways having been a member of both of them. If so I knew they would also help me.

Clay and I were selected to travel to the National FFA Convention in Louisville, Kentucky, that year. What an honor that was! Watching the National FFA Officers conduct the sessions was inspiring. They all had such a presence about them during the opening ceremonies and when they presented an award to a deserving FFA member. I was in awe and trying to take in as much as I possibly could. Clay and I kept notes and took pictures of things we wanted to take back to the chapter. We hoped it might help our members understand the depth of the organization a little better. Living so far from the mainstream of things many of our members really didn't fully understand what all the FFA had to offer.

We were also fortunate enough to take a little tour around Louisville. There were many interesting things to see and photograph. We couldn't get over the amount of water that was flowing down the Ohio River. I told Clay if we had that much water in Arizona, it would be a tropical forest. There were all sorts of boats and barges on the river. A paddle-wheel steamer even went by and Clay got a shot of it with his digital camera. After he took the photo he laughed. "I wonder if old Mark Twain is on that thing?"

When we returned from the convention, Clay and I put a Power Point presentation together with the photographs we had taken. We used our notes to develop the script. It took us forty minutes to get through it, there was so much to tell about.

Many of the members later told us they really enjoyed seeing how things actually were done at the national convention. Miss Griggs wanted us to put the power point on during the next student council meeting. It took a little convincing—but we went ahead and did it.

The holidays were just around the corner.

Mom started planning the Thanksgiving dinner. She always did that at least a month before the big day.

One day she came to me. "What do you say we invite the Billings to have Thanksgiving dinner with us?"

"That's a great idea," I replied. I knew Ginny would want to do something for her dad and brother, so I said, "Maybe Ginny would like to help you prepare the feast."

Mom liked that idea, so the next day at school I approached Clay and Ginny with Mom's suggestion. They were all for it. When they returned home after school they told their dad what Mom and I had proposed. Mr. Billings went for it right away. We would enjoy Thanksgiving together.

School let out just a couple of days before Thanksgiving. Ginny had decided to stay in town so she could help Grandmother and Mom prepare for the big Thanksgiving meal. There was a lot to keep Ginny busy: pies to bake, good china and crystal to wash and sterling to polish. The good linen napkins needed to be laundered, then starched and ironed.

Clay and I drove out to the ranch so we could help out with things. It was starting to get colder and Pete wanted to make sure all of the water lines had plenty of insulation. Ernesto and Diego were checking the pregnant cows to see whether any might calve early. As usual there was always plenty to do.

Since Pete and the kids would be in town with us for Thanksgiving, Ernesto and Diego took their families to the ranch for the day. Pete had gone into town grocery shopping a couple of days before Thanksgiving, and he'd bought turkeys for their families.

Just before we left for town on Thanksgiving morning, Ernesto and Diego brought us four dozen tamales. It was a tradition. Pete bought them turkeys and their wives sent tamales to the Billings family. The tamales really added flavor to our meal and I was sure their families enjoyed the turkeys.

The ladies really did themselves proud with the meal they had prepared for us. The table was set with Mom's best china, crystal and silver. Everything needed for a Thanksgiving feast had been prepared.

We all sat down to enjoy the meal. Mom looked at Granddad. "Dad, would you please give us a blessing?" We all held hands around the table and Granddad began. "Lord, we thank you for bringing us all together on this day of Thanksgiving. We know all that we have is through your goodness. You have blessed us to live in this fine country. You have blessed us with abundance. We are thankful for the fine meal that has been prepared by our ladies. Please bless this food that it will give us nourishment and strength. Again, thank you Lord for all you bestow upon us. In Jesus name we pray, Amen."

"Thanks, Dad," Mom said. With that the various dishes of fine food were passed around the table.

That was the first of many Thanksgivings I'd spend in Arizona. It was one I'll never forget. Both of our families had suffered greatly over the past year, but we all came together to help one another. We were all together that day to give thanks for helping us through those trying times.

When we returned back to school after our Thanksgiving break it was time to get ready for finals. I was doing well in all of my classes and seemed on the road to the Honor Roll. I really wanted to get in position for a scholarship. It was important for me to do as well as I could on tests. Clay and I studied together for the Spanish test and we both did well on it. It was up to me to prepare for my other classes on my own.

I started two weeks prior to finals, going over everything I thought would be on the exams. I must have studied the right things because I ended the quarter with a three-point eight average. It seemed to me I was on my way to securing some sort of scholarship. All I had to do was maintain that average and see what I could apply for.

Since we spent Thanksgiving in town that year Pete asked us to all come out to the ranch for Christmas. Mom thought that would be a great idea. She and Grandmother went out to decorate the place. There were brightly colored lights all over the place. Around the front porch, on the oak trees in the back yard, and even on Tobi's doghouse.

Ernesto and Diego took the Jeep to the mountains in the north pasture and brought back a six–foot pine. On Christmas Eve we had a little party and decorated it. Ginny baked at least twelve dozen cookies. She made peanut butter, chocolate chip, sugar cookies, and even little green Christmas trees with the old cookie press Grandmother showed her how to use. The colored sprinkles on top made them real pretty and Ginny was proud of her improving baking skills. She even baked a ginger bread cake.

Grandmother made hot apple cider. Mom had outdone herself making fudge, divinity and date-loaf candy. She also made colored red and green popcorn balls for everyone to enjoy. The sweet smells of Christmas filled the air. Granddad loaded the CD player with traditional Christmas carols. Those country and western singers' voices sure added to the party. It was a really festive occasion.

We all sacked out at the ranch that night. The next morning Ernesto and Diego brought their families out and we all opened presents together. Pete had bought some things for their kids. It was fun watching those little guys tear into the colorfully wrapped presents.

That evening, we had a fine meal of prime rib with all the trimmings. Again the ladies really went all out. After supper Clay pulled out his guitar, and for the first time in a long time Mr. Billings dusted off his fiddle. They played Christmas carols and all of us sang along. It was a real country Christmas.

School would be out until the first week of January. I stayed at the ranch for a few days after Christmas, but thought I should be with Mom on New Year's Eve. That was going to be a tough night for both of us. It would mark one year since Dad had been killed in Afghanistan.

I was in the tack room cleaning my saddle and getting my tack in order before I left for town. Mr. Billings walked in. "Tyler, I'd like to talk with you a little."

"Sure Mr. Billings." I replied. "Is everything okay?"

"That's what I wanted to talk with you about. Everything is better than just okay, especially considering some of the things we've all

196

experienced this past year. I just wanted to tell you how proud of you I am. I've seen you go from a kid that hardly knew anything about ranching to a fairly accomplished cattleman. You've learned a lot since you first came out here.

"I know a lot of it had to do with your FFA and 4-H activities. However, not only have you learned a lot from them, you've applied it here on the ranch. There aren't that many boys your age who take things as seriously as you have. I want you to know that wherever you go with what you're doing, I'll be behind you all the way, same as I will for Clay and Ginny. I've grown to consider you one of my own. I know Norma felt that same way before she passed away. She told me so in just so many words."

My eyes were welling up as I listened to Mr. Billings. My throat was tight and I couldn't speak. I felt like my face was turning blue from lack of oxygen. Looking up at him through tear-fogged eyes I was finally able to speak. "Mr. Billings, when I learned my dad had been killed I really didn't know what was going to happen next for Mom and me. On the trip out here in that rental truck, all I could think about was where am I going and what might be in store for me when I got there. Meeting Clay and then having Mrs. Billings and you take me in like you did was a true blessing. You've shown me many new things here on the ranch. You'll never know what this has done for me. I've learned many important lessons about life by being here with all of you. Your acceptance of my mother and the times we've all spent together mean the world to me. I'll never be able to repay you for all you've done."

He slapped me on the shoulder. "The only repayment I want is to see you become a good man and a solid citizen, no matter what profession you choose in life," Pete said with strength in his voice. He watched as I finished working on my tack. We then walked back to the house together, not saying much, just enjoying the fact we could spend time together.

I got my clothes together and walked out to my pickup. Clay walked out with me, "Listen," he said. "I know the next couple of days are goin' to be rough for you. If you need to talk, call me night or day."

"Thanks, Clay." We shook hands and I crawled into my pickup and headed to town.

Having time alone while I drove into town was therapeutic in a way. I had a Garth Brooks CD playing and my mind drifted back a couple of years to when Dad was with us. It was hard for me to believe that he would have been gone a year in just a couple of days. I knew Mom would have a difficult time New Year's Day.

As I drove along a song titled "Wolves" started

playing on the CD player. Listening to it I felt like Garth had been reading my mail. There are a lot of wolves out there in life. It seemed I'd started experiencing them that New Year's morning when we learned that Dad had been killed in action.

My thoughts began to center on my mother. *How will she handle this first anniversary of Dad's death?* I knew I had to hold myself together and be there for her. This all weighed heavily on my mind.

My grandparents were extremely supportive of Mom during that time. We all sat around their house enjoying the festivities of the holiday season. We watched some football on TV and played board games to try to keep our thoughts positive.

Mom tried to not to let it show, but I could tell she was having a difficult time. Sometimes she would leave the room and muffled sobs would come from her bedroom. When she came back into the room where we were, her eyes would be red as she wiped away the remaining tears with her handkerchief.

How we managed to make it through New Year's I'll never know. I truly believe the good Lord saw us through. Maybe Dad asked him to help us out. I don't know. All I know is that after that, things began to get better for all of us.

My classes seemed to be going my way. I was

managing to maintain some pretty good grades—good enough to make the honor roll again and be accepted into The National Honor Society. Mom was sure proud.

I was working at the ranch every weekend and my little herd was growing. That year was special during calving season. For the first time, I watched some of my calves being born. It gave new meaning to the word *responsibility*. They were *my* cattle to care for. The calves grew strong and developed well. As planned, I selected one that I thought might make a good show calf for the fair.

The calf table that Mr. Billings had given me to repair was back in working order thanks to what I had learned in shop about welding. I sold it to another member of our Ag class who needed it for his cattle project. The proceeds went to my college fund.

Clay and I were making it to some high school rodeos and doing pretty well. We both managed to increase our buckle collection. Mr. Billings had made a trophy case for the buckles I was winning. He put it next to his and Clay's at the ranch. Every time I managed to bring one home he would put it in my case. It made me feel I had accomplished one of my goals when I looked at it.

All in all my senior year was pretty successful. Both Clay and I did well in our livestock judging meets for FFA and the 4-H. We were able to do our part as chapter officers working with other members to make it a successful year.

One of the more important things we learned as officers was how to conduct a meeting using Robert's Rules of Order. Miss Griggs made us learn Parliamentary Procedure well. Not only did we use it during our meetings, we also managed to win the Parliamentary Procedure contest on the state level in Tucson at the State FFA field day.

Little did I know just how significant that would become during life. Since then I have conducted numerous meetings and been president of many organizations. What we learned in FFA regarding the proper way to conduct a meeting has been a lifelong asset.

To top it off that year I managed to get some scholastic scholarships through the FFA. Clay and I also received a rodeo scholarship at Cochise College. We looked forward to going there. They seemed to put together good teams at Cochise. Besides we'd be close to home for two years and be able to continue working at the ranch.

Chapter Nineteen
College Years

I worked at the ranch that summer after high school. Clay and I continued to take more of the work load. Mr. Billings was still having difficulties. When you're married to someone for as long as he was and then suddenly find yourself alone... well it was an extremely difficult time for him.

As I watched Mom over that year and a half, she went through what seemed like bouts of depression, loneliness and confusion. Sometimes it was like she couldn't really set a solid path for herself. She seemed to drift from one idea to another when it came to what she wanted to do in life.

Clay and Ginny seemed to put things in place somewhat easier. I knew the love that young folks had for their parents was much different than a spouse has for their mate. Mr. Billings and Mom were experiencing similar difficulties.

Clay, Ginny and I didn't discuss it much, but we could see what was going on with both of them. Knowing that, we began to assume more responsibility. We didn't make an issue of it; we just did it.

There were times Mom would drive out and

she and Ginny would prepare a nice meal for us. It seemed to help Mr. Billings when we were all at the ranch together. He seemed to relax more and enjoy everyone's company. It was plain to see that being with family and friends was very important to him.

That summer before I started college I worked hard to increase my college fund. I put almost all of my day wages in savings and only held out entry fees and travel expenses from ropings Clay and I won.

We did very well that summer and managed to win some pretty big amateur ropings. Clay also won some calf roping and bulldogging prizes that summer. We definitely improved our roping for the college rodeo team.

By summer's end I was ready to start the next phase of my education. However, I was uncertain what my degree would be in. Due to my activities in the agriculture classes the FFA and 4-H, it would definitely be something in agriculture and most likely livestock development of some type.

The first semester of college at Cochise took a little getting used to. I wasn't prepared for the freedom that I experienced. In high school our activities and time between classes were well governed by numerous regulations and time allotments. At Cochise I seemed to have more free time to study or visit.

My class schedule included the usual freshman curriculum, but I was also able to take some classes pertaining to livestock production. The agriculture department had very good classroom and shop facilities.

When it came to rodeo, the grounds were well organized. There were pipe corrals for those who had their own horses and plenty of parking for horse trailers. They also had four practice pens for timed events and bucking stock practice. It was clear that rodeo was a major part of the sports program at Cochise College.

The team had practice sessions four days a week. There were days for timed event practices and others for those who rode bulls and broncs. The school leased the livestock from local rodeo stock contractors. It was a complete program.

Most of the team lived in the dorms rather than commuting, including Clay and me. If there wasn't a college rodeo to go to, we headed back to the ranch and worked.

As the year went on I adjusted to college life pretty well. I was able to hold my grades up even with the rigorous rodeo schedule. Practice days were enjoyable. It gave me time to clear my mind and focus on something besides my classes.

When I was roping, nothing else seemed

pertinent. I just focused on roping and enjoyed what I was doing. It seemed to work. When I finished practicing I felt as though a heavy weight had been removed from my shoulders.

Our team went to seven college rodeos that year. Clay and I did well as partners in the team roping and he was leading the calf roping and bulldogging in the Grand Canyon Region.

He was almost destined to win a National Intercollegiate Championship. Clay just seemed to have that natural ability when it came to rodeo.

It was plain to see if he really put his mind to it, he would eventually get to the Professional Rodeo Cowboys Association National Finals in Las Vegas.

It was different for me. Team roping was a big part of my high school and college life, but I knew I wasn't cut out to follow the rodeo trail. Knowing this it became essential for me to decide on a major course of study, one that I would enjoy as a profession and do well with. By the end of my third semester at Cochise I had fixated on the path I would take.

Really I guess I knew what it would be all along. It just never registered until that time. Working with horses and cattle at the ranch was something I truly enjoyed. However, when I helped Mr. Billings doctor an animal that had been injured or had become sick it was extremely gratifying.

Having identified these feelings for what they really were, my goal was set. Upon graduation from Cochise College I would apply for Veterinary School at U.C. Davis in California and also Colorado State University in Ft. Collins, Colorado.

My accumulative grade point average was a three point eight nine. I had taken all of the chemistry and math that was offered at Cochise. I felt sure that I would be accepted into one of those universities.

As my fourth and final semester at Cochise College began, I decided to talk with Mr. Grover about my plans to pursue veterinary science. One day after class I asked him whether I could talk with him. He asked me to come into his office.

"Mr. Grover, I've been making plans for my transfer to a four-year university. I just thought I'd talk to you about them and get your opinion."

"Sure, Tyler," he said. "I'd be glad to hear what you have in mind. I'll help you with whatever I possibly can."

"It's like this. I moved out here to Arizona after my dad was killed in Afghanistan in 2002."

"I know," he said. "Pete Billings has told me a great deal about you. You've accomplished some great things since moving out here."

"Thanks. Up until recently, I've had a hard time deciding what I want to do after I graduate from Cochise College."

"Maybe the University of Arizona? They have a great College of Agriculture."

"Yes, Sir, they do. However, I was thinking about another route. I've been thinking of applying at U.C. Davis or Colorado State. I want to become a veterinarian."

"Wow! That's a pretty challenging path to take, that's for darn sure. To finish the courses to become a veterinarian will take you five or six more years after you leave Cochise. Are you ready for that?"

"Yes, Sir, I believe I am."

"Well, You surely have the grades and aptitude for it. You just need to know it takes dedication to go along with it."

"I've thought long and hard about this," I said. "I'm ready to go for it."

"What does your mom say about it?"

"Mom has always told me that when I decide on what I want to do in life she'll back me one hundred percent... well, as long as it's legal." I grinned.

"Tell you what," Mr. Grover said. "You fill out the applications for both of the universities and I'll write a letter of recommendation for you. I'm sure your high school agriculture teacher will as well. You're a fine young man, Tyler. I've truly enjoyed having you in my classes. You always worked hard, not to mention your dedication to the rodeo team."

"Thank you, Mr. Grover. That truly means a great deal to me coming from you."

"Let me know how you're doing on the applications. If you need any help, holler. In the meantime I'll work up those letters for you."

I put the applications together and made arrangements for my transcripts from Douglas High School and Cochise College to be sent to both universities. Mr. Grover provided me with letters of recommendation, as did Miss. Griggs. All of the documents were completed and sent. Now the waiting game was on. Would I be accepted at one of the universities?

My final semester at Cochise College seemed to pass by quickly. Clay and I continued going to ropings as well as to college rodeos with the team. Our team did well that year and managed to make it to the college finals.

As expected Clay won the National Intercollegiate Championship in bulldogging and placed second in the calf roping. We did well as a team and ended up third in the Grand Canyon Region.

The scholastic and rodeo scholarships I received in high school really helped me through my first two years at Cochise College. Now I had to prepare for the university. If I made it into veterinary school I'd really need some financial assistance.

Clay had applied to the University of Arizona. He was accepted into the College of Agriculture. He wanted to study livestock production and range management. That was probably a pretty good decision on his part. He was able to get back to the ranch whenever he had a break. Mr. Billings was getting back to his normal self and Clay could continue to help him through some of his tougher times.

As I waited for answers from U.C. Davis and Colorado State, I continued working at the ranch and spending time with my grandparents in Douglas. The more I was around them the more I realized how fortunate I was to have had them as grandparents. They had gone through a number of trials during their life together. Listening to them only made me more determined to accomplish my goals.

At long last I heard from U.C. Irvine and a week later Colorado State. It was a thrill to find that both of them had accepted my application. The hard work I had put in at Douglas High and Cochise College had paid off, and my participation in the agriculture programs of FFA and 4-H had boosted my understanding of what I wanted to pursue in life.

Now it was up to me to make the critical decision as to which university to attend. It would be a hard decision for me to make, so I decided to talk it over with those who had mentored me. First I had a pow-wow with Mom and my grandparents, then Mr. Billings.

Miss Griggs and Mr. Glover were helpful in that they gave me information about both schools. It seemed none of those I spoke with wanted to make the decision for me. I had come this far, and the final decision should be mine. After careful consideration I decided to go to Colorado State.

Our big night arrived. It marked the successful completion of two years of higher education. Clay and I were thrilled, as were Mom and Mr. Billings. We were probably the only two graduates wearing Wranglers and boots under our graduation gown. When I looked at that diploma I knew it was only the beginning.

Mom and Mr. Billings seemed relaxed that evening. I hadn't seen either of them like that in more than a year. They laughed and joked and kidded each other about Clay and me. It was great seeing them enjoy themselves. It was like they had reached a new place in their lives, and they were once again able to enjoy the moment.

That summer, as fate would have it, Mom began to spend more time at the ranch. She even started riding and would accompany us when we all checked cattle. She was becoming quite adapted to ranch life, even more so than she had been while caring for Mrs. Billings. She and Ginny were becoming dependent on one another and I could see that Ginny confided in mom a great deal.

Time was growing near for Clay and me to head to our respective universities. I didn't realize just how difficult that would be. We had become like brothers ever since that first day at Douglas High when we'd met in the cafeteria. I wasn't looking forward to us not being able to work and rope together. I would miss him when we left for school.

I'll never forget the little meeting Mom and Mr. Billings had with the three of us. Clay and I had pretty much prepared for our departures. We were all sitting in the living room at the ranch. Ginny and Mom were doing some sort of embroidery work, Clay was reading a rodeo sports news magazine and I was just looking around and thinking about how far things had come over the past three and a half years.

Looking at the three trophy cases full of buckles I thought back to the first day I'd walked into that living room. Seeing the two cases holding Mr. Billings' and Clay's buckles became the gold ring on the merry-go-round. How I wanted to win one of those sterling silver buckles. Thanks to them I had won a number of them, and a couple of saddles as well. I owed so much to them. How would I ever be able to thank them enough?

About that time Mr. Billings put down his stockman report and glanced around at us all, then looked straight at me as if to gain my approval, although for what I had no idea. "I have something to say to ya'll."

We all looked at him, not saying a word. He seemed so serious.

Mr. Billings cleared his throat. "You kids have endured a great deal in your lives, more than most kids will ever have to go through. But you've done well for yourselves thanks to your effort in the various organizations you've been involved with." He paused.

Mom said, "And thanks to what you've done for them Pete."

He smiled at her, then said, "Y'know, there are a number of paths a person can take when they have things happen that aren't pleasant in life, especially young folks. But as I was saying, your FFA and 4-H activities really kept you on a positive path. I'm sure there are activities out there for others that don't have those organizations to participate in, but you took advantage of what you had. I just want you to know how proud I am of what you've all accomplished."

Mom looked at him. "Pete, is there something else you want to say to the kids?"

Mr. Billings got up and walked around the room. He stopped. Then, shuffling his feet, he said, "Well, yes there is. Katherine and I have grown quite close this past summer." He paused, then said, "Well, it's like this... I've asked Katherine to marry me."

Silence overtook the room. Clay, Ginny and I looked at each other with blank stares, trying to digest what we had just been told.

"No foolin'!" I blurted out. "You're going to get married?"

"Yes," Mom replied. "Yes we are."

Clay stumbled into the conversation. "When?"

Mr. Billings said, "Well, we want to get married during your Thanksgiving break from school. Kay and I thought that would be just one more thing to be thankful for this year."

"Wow!" Ginny walked over and put her arms around Mom. "This is wonderful news!"

Clay and I looked at each other. Then smiled. "Well, howdy Brother."

We both gave Pete a hug.

Clay said, "Dad, Ginny and I couldn't ask for anything better. We want you to be happy and I'm sure Mrs. Roland will make sure you are."

Pete replied happily, "Thanks, Clay." Then he

looked at me. "Tyler, please, from now on call me Dad if you want to, not Mr. Billings."

Mom chimed in. "That goes for the two of you as well. It's Mom, not Mrs. Roland."

That was a day none of us will ever forget.

The day finally came that I left for Colorado State. I wouldn't be back until Thanksgiving break. At that point my future seemed brighter. However, there was still a certain amount of uncertainty. Could I accomplish my goal? Only time and hard work would tell.

After living in Arizona for the past three and a half years, I found Colorado to be a culture shock. School wasn't that much different—I had been in many schools growing up and I always adapted quickly to my new surroundings—but the weather was a shock. I'd never lived in an area that had this much snow in the winter, and the freezing cold was sometimes more than I thought I could take. There were days I thought I'd freeze to death.

One day I decided to get a haircut. The weather was brutal that day. As I sat waiting my turn in the barber chair, I noticed a poster on the wall. It was advertising their tanning salon in the basement. While getting my haircut I inquired as to what the tanning sessions cost.

When I heard the price per month I was sold. I

went on a regular basis. At long last I found a place where I could warm up for awhile.

I did manage to get work in the Animal Husbandry Department. The pay was okay, and with the money I'd saved from working at the ranch and selling my calves I managed.

Rodeo wasn't in the cards for me that first semester. I concentrated on my classes and work. Some of my classes were much more demanding than those at Cochise College, so I had to put a great deal of time into studying.

My job also required a lot of attention. There were nights I had to assist with a medical procedure that was being performed. Sometimes it would last well into the early morning hours. Time became a valuable commodity. Learning how to use it well became an asset.

My main goal in life was to get through veterinary school. Having graduated from two years of college at Cochise, four more years were ahead of me. I knew it would be an arduous undertaking.

Mom and Mr. Billings were married that Thanksgiving. It was quite an event. They had decided to have the ceremony at the ranch. People came from almost every western state. I met folks I'd never seen before.

Pete, having been on the rodeo circuit in his

younger days, had friends all over the west. All of his neighbors in the ranching community were there as well as folks from many of the towns in Cochise County.

I never would have believed it, but Chaplain Beeler had taken leave and flown out to perform the wedding ceremony. He even had on a new western suit, hat and boots. That was a far cry from what he was wearing the last time I saw him. Back then he'd had on BDU's, bloused jump boots and a Green Beret.

Ginny was maid of honor and Pete had asked me to be his best man. Clay along with Ernesto and Diego took on the responsibility of getting people seated.

Ernesto and Diego's wives prepared a buffet of just about everything imaginable. What a feast that was, with prime rib, turkey and the trimmings and of course a huge batch of tamales. Grandmother and the Cowbelles provided cakes and pies of all kinds.

After the ceremony and meal a band called the Rocking R Drifters played and folks danced up a storm. It was one of the finest events I'd ever experienced.

Clay and I headed back to our respective universities. Clay completed his Bachelor of Science Degree in Livestock Production with a minor in Range Management over the next two and a half years. He also hit the rodeo trail a little and almost qualified for the National Finals Rodeo in Las Vegas. He was running at 'em pretty hard in the calf roping and dogging. However, once he graduated he went back to the ranch. Like Pete, he became dedicated to the ranch.

Chapter Twenty
Dr. Tyler Roland, D.V.M.

It took me what seemed like forever to get through my studies in Veterinary Science. I managed to finish by the end of the spring semester of 2010. Pete, Mom and Ginny flew up to Colorado for graduation. It sure was nice to see them again.

After the graduation ceremony we had supper at a real nice steak house. Pete got right to the point. "Tyler, what do you have in mind now? Are you going to come back to Arizona, or do you have something else you want to do?"

"I've thought a great deal about that." I said. "If it's okay with you, I'd like to go back to the ranch. I've thought about starting a mobile practice in Cochise County. That way I can also help out at the ranch. What do you think?"

"I told you one time, I'd back you in whatever you decided to do in life. Honestly it thrills me that you want to come home. I know you'll be successful in that part of Arizona."

I looked at Mom. "Mom, what do you think of the idea?"

"You know it would make me very happy to have you back home. I'm with Pete on this. Whatever you decide to do, I'm for it."

The next day I drove them to the Denver

airport. They boarded and I watched the big plane take to the sky. It had been a rewarding visit. Knowing there was a long trip back to the ranch ahead of me, I wasted no time getting everything packed and in my pickup.

The next morning I headed south. Within six hours I crossed into New Mexico and headed for Southern Arizona. The closer I got to the ranch, the more confident of my decision I became.

My practice developed at a steady pace. Before I knew it I had clients all over Cochise and Eastern Santa Cruz Counties. Everything was going well.

Now there I was—standing in the stall looking at a two year old colt that had just slammed me against the wall, ringing my bell. I was dazed. I'd considered all the events of my life that had brought me to this train wreck.

I heard a familiar voice say, "There are a lot of things in life that don't seem fair. We just have to make the most of what we have. Do things with strength, courage and determination and soon your future will be manifested."

Trying to regain my senses, I looked around the stall. I knew that Master Sergeant Roland had to be there somewhere. Of course, he was nowhere to be seen. I looked up, grinned and shook my head. "Thanks, Dad."

Then I finished doctoring that stubborn colt.

About the Author

John William Mangum was born in the small northern New Mexico village of Pecos. While his father was serving in the Philippine Islands during World War II, John was relocated to Southern Arizona where he lived with his grandparents on their ranch. John's grandfather, D.C. Mangum, was instrumental in cultivating his interests in ranch life.

In his youth John spent a great deal of time helping friends on their ranches as well as owning cattle and horses of his own. Once in high school John enrolled in agriculture classes and joined the Future Farmers of America eventually serving as chapter president and then as an Arizona State F.F.A. Vice-President. During this time he also participated in high school rodeo, riding bulls, team roping and also played guitar in a small country band.

During the Vietnam Conflict John served in the United States Army Special Forces (Airborne), better known as The Green Berets, as a demolition engineer on an "A Team". On returning home he attended college, graduating from Cochise College with an Associate of Arts Degree in Business. And then went on to obtain a Bachelor of Arts Degree from Arizona State University in History and Secondary Education.

John now lives in Southern Arizona, where he writes and raises Quarter Horses. They are used for team roping, mounted shooting, bulldogging, barrel racing and racing. He is a licensed racehorse owner / trainer.

Inspired by his studies in history and his many and varied life experiences John say's "What I write is partly truth and partly fiction. The names have been changed to protect the guilty. You know who you are."

www.ingramcontent.com/pod-product-compliance
Lightning Source LLC
Chambersburg PA
CBHW050928120626
46552CB00001B/93